THE WOLVES ARE WATCHING

Also available by Victoria Houston

The Lew Ferris Mysteries

At the Edge of the Woods
Hidden in the Pines
Wolf Hollow

The Loon Lake Fishing Mysteries

Dead Big Dawg
Dead Firefly
Dead Spider
Dead Loudmouth
Dead Rapunzel
Dead Lil' Hustler
Dead Insider
Dead Tease
Dead Deceiver
Dead Renegade
Dead Hot Shot
Dead Madonna
Dead Boogie
Dead Jitterbug
Dead Hot Mama
Dead Frenzy
Dead Water
Dead Creek
Dead Angler

Nonfiction Titles

Michelle and Me
Restore Yourself
My Health History
Making It Work
Loving a Younger Man
Alone After School
Self-Care for Kids

THE WOLVES ARE WATCHING

A LEW FERRIS MYSTERY

VICTORIA HOUSTON

NEW YORK

Books should be disposed of and recycled according to local requirements.
All paper materials used are FSC compliant.

This is a work of fiction. All of the names, characters, organizations, places and events portrayed in this novel are either products of the author's imagination or are used fictitiously. Any resemblance to real or actual events, locales, or persons, living or dead, is entirely coincidental.

Published in the United States by Crooked Lane Books, an imprint of
The Quick Brown Fox & Company LLC.

Crooked Lane Books and its logo are trademarks of The Quick Brown Fox & Company LLC.

Library of Congress Catalog-in-Publication data available upon request.

ISBN (hardcover): 979-8-89242-426-4
ISBN (paperback): 979-8-89242-427-1
ISBN (ebook): 979-8-89242-428-8

Cover design by Nebosja Zoric

Printed in the United States.

www.crookedlanebooks.com

Crooked Lane Books
34 West 27th St., 10th Floor
New York, NY 10001

First Edition: February 2026

The authorized representative in the EU for product safety and compliance is eucomply OÜPärnu mnt 139b-14, 11317 Tallinn, Estonia,
hello@eucompliancepartner.com, +33757690241

10 9 8 7 6 5 4 3 2 1

For Mike

PROLOGUE

THE BOARD OF directors for the Crossroads Chapter of Wolf Watchers had started their meeting before their former president Dr. John McKenzie had arrived, and that irritated him.

"What the hell? You can't wait five minutes?" he said, muttering as he pulled a chair out to join the group. His wife, who had followed him into the room, spotted a chair in the corner and sat down quietly.

"Hello, Miriam," said one of the men at the table next to John's wife, his voice kind, in contrast to her husband's huffing and puffing.

John McKenzie had been president of the group for two years, but two years of his belligerence and demanding that everyone follow his orders had been enough, and he no longer led the group.

"We're volunteers," Harry Onson had said at the time, "we are not your staff—"

"—or your wife," another group member had added.

Watching the board members this morning, Miriam understood their frustrations. The last time the group held a wolf-watching session up in Door County, John had assigned every person a position and made it clear they had to stay in that spot. "You set up your telescopes and cameras and don't move or you will mess up someone else's view."

"But I never see anything move," one man had protested. His wife agreed but John had been adamant. The couple clearly was not happy—they knew they would not be assigned a prime location.

His wife was aware that John, of course, would not hesitate to assign less desirable locations to people he didn't like—or those who complained.

"I tell you where your spot is, and don't you move," he would insist.

Miriam knew their frustration, as she experienced it daily. She had married John over forty years earlier when both were just out of school—her with a new nursing degree and John just starting his residency as a surgeon, and married life seemed new and exciting. Two years into the marriage, she knew she had made the mistake of marrying a bully, but it was too late: they had a young son on the way. Over the years, she learned how to duck and weave, handling her husband's demands in ways that kept him happy and her relatively content, and let their son thrive. And she hadn't said a word as new hires—nurses, assistants, other doctors—to his office staff would often leave after less than a year of dealing with his rude approach to running a medical practice.

The only time she had ever seen him back off from a confrontation had, oddly enough, happened the first time they had joined a Wolf Watchers group on a day of watching a wolf pack up in Door County. On arriving early that day, they had left their lunch in their car, which was parked about a third of a mile from the wolf-watching site. Toward noon that day, John had decided to walk back and get it. On the path leading to where they had parked, he had seen a lone wolf. The animal was less that fifty feet away and standing still watching John. Later, John would tell Miriam, "I shouted at him and lurched forward, thinking that would scare him off. But, no, that damn wolf just stood there staring at me."

And so, John admitted grudgingly, " I backed off. I had to. That's why I told you to forget lunch that day. I knew better than to challenge that guy." After telling her the story of his encounter, John had chuckled.

John may have chuckled, but Miriam knew the reality was not humorous: Dr. John McKenzie had met his match and lost. Was it any wonder that from that confrontation on the path that day that he became a fanatic wolf watcher, always buying the best equipment, always wanting the best viewing spots?

Today was not going well. She wasn't sure what, if anything, she could do to calm down the board members—much less her husband.

Closing in on seventy now, Miriam McKenzie was a good-looking woman. Tall and somewhat heavy with the weight of her years, she had a fair complexion and a remarkable lack of wrinkles given her age. She wore her white-blond hair in a soft wispy bun held in place with a black plastic comb. The fact was John was good-looking, too—and knew it—and they had always made an attractive couple . . . until John felt the need to be boss.

It was Harry Onson who had made the move to unseat John as president of the Crossroads Board and it was Harry who seemed to make it a point to needle John whenever he could. Yes, John was an MD and head of the primary care team at their local clinic, but Harry had made millions running a large accounting practice and investing in real estate. In his world, working in health care could never trump large amounts of cash in the bank. And he seemed to enjoy reminding John of that.

At the moment, the board was focused on their upcoming week of wolf watching. Plans had to be detailed with everyone's location specified, lodgings arranged, and equipment organized. The idea was to have a remarkable experience spotting and watching the elusive wolves and to enjoy the outdoors and one another: husbands, wives, et al. At least that was what Miriam was hoping, but already John had been making noises about quitting the group. That would break her heart, as she thoroughly enjoyed the outings and the men and women in the group.

After the board meeting, Miriam took her husband aside. "Really, John, don't let Harry get to you. He has too much fun when you get upset."

"Oh, shut up, Miriam. I know what I'm doing. If he gets in the way of my having my prime viewing location, I will personally have him kicked out of Crossroads."

"I don't think you can do that, John."

"Oh, yeah?" His tone was belligerent, and Miriam knew to drop it. Her husband always had to have the last word

Late the next week, on the afternoon when John and Miriam arrived up north, they rushed to drop their suitcases at the inn where everyone was staying, then hurried out to the wolf-watching area. No one had taken the spot John insisted was his, which relieved Miriam's anxiety. She helped him unload and set up their gear. When it was ready, John took his position for viewing. Miriam, meanwhile, settled into the folding chair nearby. *Whew*, she was thinking, relieved that John was happy and she could enjoy the day.

Then her world exploded.

"He's taken over my views to the east—my priceless early morning view! My whole reason for working with these stupid people!" John's voice was so loud that anything alive within five miles would have heard him, not so great for watching wildlife. But before Miriam could say a word, much less stand up from where she was sitting, John was marching down the slight hill where they were situated and disappearing into a stand of aspen.

Sounds of something metal and glass being smashed or shattered echoed from beyond the trees. Although shocked, Miriam didn't have to ask if her husband was the culprit—of course it was John. What she did wonder was if he would be arrested.

"Hurry, Miriam," shouted John a few minutes later, coming into view at the bottom of the hill. "We have to get out of here."

Later, she dared to ask him a question. "How much was Harry's equipment worth, do you think?"

"You mean the stuff I smashed?"

She nodded.

"Maybe ten grand."

Maybe more, thought Miriam, *and maybe he's not going to let you get away with ruining his equipment and his wolf watching this trip*. She hated being a part of this; she was ashamed of her husband and felt like a criminal fleeing the scene. But what could she do?

And what would come later? Would they be thrown out of the group? *Almost certainly*, she thought with a sick feeling. Would Harry press charges? Would John be arrested? She inwardly cringed, and wondered what they would tell their adult son, Brian, and his wife. What would an arrest do to John's temperament? To his medical practice? She shuddered at the thought.

CHAPTER

1

BEN FOUND A smooth grassy spot on the bank of the trout stream where he could roll out his sleeping bag and watch the moon draw circles through the riffles in the middle of the stream. The murmur of the flowing water lulled him to sleep only to have something—a noise?—jar him awake.

Turning onto his side, the teenager glanced back towards where he had left his bicycle standing against a large boulder. Neon blue eyes were staring at him, two sets of them. Four neon blue eyes. Wolves.

He lay still. The eyes did not move. He looked away, turned over and got to his knees. Without looking toward the boulder, he rolled up the sleeping bag, pulled on his tennis shoes and got to his feet. Only then, his breath still held, did he look—no eyes. The animals were gone.

An hour later, he pedaled up the driveway to his dad's house in the dark, parked his bike against the garage in his usual spot and crept in the side door and up the stairs to his bedroom. Once in his bed, he felt he could breathe. With a deep inhale, he closed his eyes. Safe.

His eyes were still closed when he heard his father's voice. "Ben," said the tall figure in the doorway, "I've been worried sick. Why? What is wrong? Why did you take off?" He felt his dad sit down beside him on the bed. "Thank God you're back." A hand brushed the hair on his head. "We'll talk in the morning . . . okay?"

Ben nodded. It would be hard to tell his father what had happened, what had scared him so, but he knew he needed to.

CHAPTER

2

ROB MASON CLOSED his bedroom door and called his close friend, who had been coaching his son's high school muskie fishing group. He knew Ray was as worried as he was.

"He's home," was all he said.

"Thank God," said Ray. "Did he say where he's been, or why he took off?"

"Not a word. The look on his face—I know he doesn't want to talk about it. I just let him go to bed."

"This is so strange. I just can't imagine. I mean, his team is one tournament away from winning a hundred thousand dollars this coming Saturday—it's an odd time to just take off. That's huge money for high school kids."

"You don't have to tell me," Rob said, "and I know Ben knows that, too."

A long pause. "Rob, any chance there's a girl involved in this?"

"I don't know. No idea. All I can say is I'm his dad and he doesn't talk to me. What's your morning like? Maybe you can get it out of him. . . ."

"I'll sure try. Right now, I'm happy he's alive and safe."

"Goddamn right. Okay, we'll deal with it in the morning."

* * *

Lew's first mistake that morning was enjoying the early autumn sunlight shimmering in the dew on the newly planted shrubs outside her office window. She still missed the sight of elegant oaks that had graced the views from the Loon Lake Police Department. Being sheriff had its benefits, but working in the company of glorious, ancient trees wasn't one of them. Her offices now were in a new building, a building without character and lacking the resonance of history.

"Oh, well, I'll find something to appreciate," she would remind herself, time after time. She was still working on it.

Her second mistake was answering the phone.

"Sheriff Ferris—you have a call from the state patrol that I'm sure you want to take," said Marlaine from Dispatch.

"Is this going to ruin my day?" Lew asked with a low chortle.

"Yep," said Marlaine. Lew could hear her smile. And she knew Marlaine had to be right. Twenty-plus years of working together meant the switchboard operator's instincts were as good as her own.

"Put 'em through," said Lew with a sigh and one final glance at the sun-dappled leaves.

"Need your help, Chief Ferris," said the brusque but friendly male voice. "Calling you from down here near Milwaukee. We got a couple—a man and his wife in their sixties—who've gone missing up in your area."

Lew pulled over her notepad. "Who says they're missing?"

"Their son and his wife. I've confirmed they have good reason to worry. No response to calls to their cell phones, no text messages returned, and they did not arrive at the lodge where they had booked a week-long stay. No sign of their vehicle. Are you familiar with the Wolf Watchers club?"

"Yes, of course." Lew knew there was a national organization of wolf watchers, based in Duluth, and that members of the club were devoted to spotting and observing wolves in the wild, using powerful scopes to study them. "They hold an annual fundraiser over in Rhinelander every spring. Do I assume these two are members?"

"Yes, and they had planned to spend this coming week watching wolves in your backyard. Well, not *your* backyard but you know what I mean."

"Where exactly?" asked Lew. The urgency in his voice made her determined to narrow the search as quickly as possible. As she listened, she buzzed Dani Wright, the department's IT specialist.

He answered quickly. "I don't have an exact location but their family thinks they were hoping to find a good spot somewhere east of Rhinelander but closer to Loon Lake, which is about thirty miles from where they have a family cabin. Their son drove up there late last night but found no sign of them. He called us around midnight. I have six troopers working the area, including attempts to track their phones, which has failed and *that*, Sheriff Ferris, is not a good sign."

"Give me the approximate coordinates and I'll have deputies heading that way ASAP. And their son's name and cell number. He's still up here, right? I'll touch base with him to see what locations he's scouted."

Dani walked into Lew's office and sat down, listening while Lew finished talking with the State Patrol. Lew put herself on speaker to call the missing couple's son, whose name was Brian McKenzie. After telling him why she had him on speaker, Lew said, "I know this is a hard time for you, Brian, and I'll have deputies out there to help your search shortly but right now my IT manager and I need to know what you know for a detailed search through our tech options, some of which are excellent out in the field."

Once he had described what he knew from his parents and where he and the troopers had been searching, Lew said, "Good, Brian, that's all we need. I'll text you whom to expect out there within a half hour at most."

She turned to Dani after clicking off her phone. "Assuming you had no luck," she said.

Dani had Google Maps up on the large laptop she had brought into the room. "Take a look. Can you see okay, Sheriff?" asked Dani as she angled her chair so they could share the view.

"Yes." The room was quiet as Dani scrolled over the areas that Brian McKenzie had described on the phone. They saw the troopers' cars and figures moving, though they were often hidden in the trees.

"I don't know that area that well," said Dani in a low voice. "Do you?"

Lew wasn't surprised. Dani had never planned for a career in law enforcement. She had been in the Loon Lake Community College Cosmetology program with an emphasis on makeup, nails, and hair when Lew discovered by total accident that the young woman had a natural talent for IT work.

At the time, Lew had been deep into a criminal investigation of a murder than had taken place near the local community college when a lack of regional tech support for the Loon Lake Police Department had stymied her. Randomly begging for "anyone who knows the Internet, for God's sake" had prompted a young woman to volunteer, saying she "might be able to help. . . ." The young student was Dani Wright. And her efforts led to a major break in the case.

Aiming at opening her own hair salon, Dani was, at first, taken aback when Lew offered her a part-time position at the Loon Lake Police Department. Once she realized Lew was right—that she was a natural talent in the universe of IT—she changed her mind and decided to abandon her plans of having a hair salon, to earn a salary, and instead of making a living doing hair and nails, to spend her IT income on having her *own* hair and nails done.

Sitting silent alongside Dani, her eyes fixed on the screen, Lew thought about what she knew about wolves in her area. Once nearly vanished from the state, in the last sixty years the wolf population, now protected from hunting, had grown, especially in the forested northern areas, until there were an estimated thousand wolves in her state and multiple wolf packs. And she knew from fly fishing streams in the area that there were six wolf packs in McBride County. As she studied the images captured by Google Maps, she had the sense, oddly enough, that she was looking at a familiar face. "Not a face, idiot," she told herself, "a *place.* You know this place. . . ." Then it hit her: they were studying the woods and shoreline close to the expensive, sprawling country house owned by Ray Pradt's parents.

Ray was familiar to Lew for reasons good and bad. She had encountered him shortly after joining the Loon Lake Police Department when she had to arrest him for growing marijuana behind his father's hunting shack. Struck by his honesty and willingness to live by the rules of his misdemeanor sentence, she found him an engaging young guy: good-looking, full of inappropriate jokes, but a gifted outdoorsman. In his early teens he had befriended two elders with the local

Ojibwa tribe who taught him the secrets of tracking deer and mink, not to mention people. He was still in his teens when he realized the forests and the lakes were his true home. Was it a talent or a skill that he could sense the presence of a prize muskie or delicious walleye just beneath the surface of one of the Northwoods lakes? He never knew and he never questioned but by his mid-twenties he found himself in demand as one of the most sought-after fishing guides in the state.

Even so, in a perverse twist of fate, Ray's willingness to experiment led to an early—too early—descent into alcoholism, which led to an equally early stint in rehab. While he may have been one of the youngest people to find their way to the Hazelden/Betty Ford Drug and Alcohol Treatment Center, he made the choice to stay sober. However, sober as he might be, he didn't drop his friendships with buddies who were not so inclined—the people Lew often referred to as "bad actors who live down roads with no fire numbers." In other words, Ray's sobriety did not get in the way of knowing people who might hold clues to who and where unlawful activity might take place. Lew could see that it worked both ways—Ray enjoyed people regardless of their attitude (or record) toward the law and those same people found him a willing, agreeable listener.

Bottom line: over time, whether searching for drug dealers or lost children, he had proven to be a valuable undercover deputy—one of Lew's best assets.

* * *

"Oh gosh, Dani," Lew exclaimed. "You know who really knows this area? Ray. This is where he grew up! If anyone knows where a wolf pack might have a den, it's Ray!"

"What are you waiting for?" asked Dani without taking her eyes off the screen. "I sure have no idea where a wolf den might be."

"I couldn't spot one either," said Lew as she was punching Ray's number into her personal cell phone.

At first, there was no answer. Then she heard Ray's voice but what followed sure didn't sound like the wise-cracking Ray Pradt she knew.

CHAPTER 3

RAY GOT TO Rob's house five minutes before eight that morning. "Shh, Ben's still asleep," said the teen's father, keeping his voice low as he opened the side door to his small wood-frame house. "Coffee?"

"Of course," said Ray, trying to smile as he stepped into the kitchen. Once he had a full mug of coffee in hand, he turned to his friend, a well-known entomologist. "I'm confused, Rob," he said, "all summer your son has seemed to be not just happy but committed to winning the final trophy. He and the other boys work well together, they take direction great, and you know, they laugh at my crazy jokes. Taking off like that? I don't get it . . . although . . . could this have anything to do with losing his mother?"

"Maybe," said Rob, "but Carolyn has been gone a year now. He and I have talked about her cancer and how lonely we've been since she died but. . . . I don't think so. It's something else and it happened recently. Two days ago Ben was fine. We had dinner at the Loon Lake Pub and had a great talk about where he'd like to go to college." Rob raised his eyebrows. "Like maybe somewhere other than where his old man is teaching. Yeah, I don't know what this is all about."

He set his coffee mug down, crossed his legs and stared down at the moccasin on his right foot. "So up until two days ago, I had no sense that anything was wrong with him. Nothing," he repeated. "And I know my son."

"I took on coaching because I really like the boys—all five of 'em," said Ray. "I mean, you have to be nuts to agree to coach a bunch of kids competing in muskie tournaments. But they've been great. They've worked hard all summer and fished in eleven tournaments. Eleven! And now they get to compete in a final for *a hundred thousand dollars*."

"Are you kidding? That much?" Rob's eyes widened. "I don't think Ben has ever thought they would make it this far. I do know he has been impressed with you as his coach." Rob gave a soft laugh. "He's always said he wants to do what I do—be a professor of entomology so he can work outdoors—but now he wants to be a professional muskie guy—like you! Guess a hundred grand makes a difference, huh?"

Ray had been asked to coach by the boys themselves because they had heard from their friends' fathers how Ray wasn't just a fisherman with a talent for selecting the right lure at the right time, but had an uncanny ability to read water. The local legend was that he could "sense" when a fish would rise, hungry and ready to strike. And so the boys had asked him to be their coach, teach them his secrets and, if they won, share in the prize.

What they didn't know was that intuitive as Ray might be to the wiles of the muskie, he was just as tuned in to the behaviors of the humans around him: good, bad, and weird. Right now he was finding the behavior of young Ben to be very odd, and out of character. And he wanted to find out what the problem was. And the teen's father did too.

"Ray," said Rob, keeping his voice low, "my son will listen to you, way better than me. I know he thinks you're brilliant in the boat—stop, let me finish," he said, waving away Ray's expression of embarrassment. "And he respects your opinion. He's shared some of the things you've talked about with the boys—about girls, about life, y'know. Right now, he might just listen to you better than me."

With that, Rob got to his feet and speaking in a louder voice, he said, "I have something to fix in the garage for a few minutes, Ray. I'll be back. Help yourself to more coffee."

Ray sat quiet at the kitchen table, thinking about the hundred thousand dollars. He hadn't expected the boys to qualify either. But they had, and with that had come the specter of another issue that he hadn't discussed with the boys, one that adult teams were struggling to deal with: sports betting.

Gambling, even though it was technically illegal in Wisconsin, had infiltrated the fishing sports just as it had the world of more mainstream sports—football, baseball, soccer, tennis. But teenage muskie fishing? Absurd as it felt to him, Ray knew it wasn't hugely far-fetched. He thought of the men with whom he was familiar who had just been caught cheating in walleye fishing tournaments—deliberately fixing the results. With a heart-hurting thud, he sensed in an instant what might have happened to Ben. *Someone may have offered him a bribe to throw the competition.* But why wouldn't he have just come to Ray or to his father?

After about five minutes, he stood up and walked down the hallway that his friend had gestured to that led to the bedrooms. One door was open and the double bed inside neatly made—that had to be Rob's room, one he had shared with his late wife. The other door was closed. Ray tapped on it, then nudged it open to peer in. The teenager on the bed was wide awake, staring back at him. Neither said a word for a long moment.

Then Ray spoke. "I know," he said in a low, friendly tone. "I know what happened." The boy's eyes darted away at first, then he looked back at his coach with a barely perceptible nod. "I'll be in the kitchen, Ben. Come tell me about it."

Back in the kitchen, Ray was refilling his coffee mug when his cell phone rang. "I can't talk right now," he said before the person calling could say a word.

After a confused pause, his friend Lew Ferris spoke anyway. "I need your help badly," she said. "Two older people who are missing may be lost on property near your parents' home. How soon can you call me back?"

"Call my dad, he's home."

Another pause. "He doesn't know what you know."

"I'll call you back in an hour." The phone clicked off.

Lew stared at the cell phone in her hand. This was not the Ray Pradt she knew. When was the last time he had answered without making her listen to one of his stupid politically incorrect jokes? Or insisted she let him drop off a fresh catch of bluegills? Or, truly, be willing to listen to why she was calling? Or passed up the chance to help with a case?

Had she reached Ray or accidentally called someone else? She checked the number. Of course she had called Ray. How strange—had someone else answered the phone. But no, the voice, while distant, had been Ray's. She walked out to climb into her cruiser, still shaking her head. Unsure whom to assign the search to, in the meantime she decided to meet with the state troopers at the site she'd been given and hope Ray called back soon.

CHAPTER

4

BEN WALKED INTO the kitchen and sat at the kitchen table across from Ray. He didn't say anything.

"I ran away from home, once, Ben—when I was in the seventh grade," said Ray, "so I know sometimes that seems like the only answer. 'Course, I was gone only one night. Then I crawled home and took my punishment."

"Really? What did you do?"

"You mean why did I take off?"

Ben nodded.

"I got kicked out of St. Mary's school for two weeks after I put a jar of leeches in my girlfriend's desk. Well, she wasn't my girlfriend but I had a crush on her. I thought she would think it was funny and we could, y'know, get along. But no one thought it was funny."

Ben chuckled. "So you were goofy even then?"

"Yep."

Ben stared down at the tabletop. After a moment he spoke. "I wasn't goofy . . . I was scared."

"Ah," said Ray, "tell me about it and it can be our secret."

Ben heaved a heavy sigh, twisted in his chair, then said, "This guy came up to me when I was buying minnows the day before yesterday. . . ."

"Where was this?"

"At Ralph's," he said, referring to Ralph's Sporting Goods, a local store. "He said he had been watching me fishing these last tournaments and knew how I could make a couple thousand bucks."

"Ah," said Ray again. "I figured it had to be something like this."

"Yeah, he would pay me if I fake my catch the first or second day, so guys betting can make money."

Ray knew this could be done: the fisher could "fudge" the measurements or not report some fish. "Yep. What made you decide not to do that?"

Ben gave Ray a long sad look, almost as if he was disappointed in Ray. "I would never do that. It would let down my teammates and would be just wrong—plus my dad would be so disappointed in me. That's not what we do in our family. My mom. . . . I can't cheat like that, but the guy really scared me."

"He *scared* you?" Ray straightened up in his chair. "He threatened you?"

"It's more that he threatened my dad. He said if I didn't do it, he would see that my dad lost the grants that pay for his research. He said his family donates millions of dollars to the university for Dad's work and he could put a stop to that."

"I think he's full of baloney." Ray kept his voice even. He wanted as much info as he could get out of Ben. "So he made it sound—"

"Like if I didn't do what he wanted me to, Dad would lose his job."

"Why did you take off? I wish you had told your dad or called me."

Ben broke into tears. "I . . . I was scared. The guy was so . . . so mean, I felt like he would hurt me or hurt my dad. I thought it might be easier if I just disappeared and missed the tournament." Ben closed his eyes and shook his head. "I know it doesn't make sense but ever since Mom died, I have been so worried for my dad. His work is all he has, y'know?"

And the boy sobbed. Ray sat, waiting.

When Ben lifted his head, Ray said, "What was his name? This creep."

"He didn't tell me."

"Okay, I'll find out whose family donates that kind of money and we'll know the family he referred to—if that's true. He was probably making all that up. What does he look like?"

"Maybe in his forties? Or fifties? I don't know. He was white. Dark hair, not long. Not tall but he's got muscle."

"Any facial hair? Glasses? Tattoos or anything?

Ben shook his head. "Not that I noticed. Just pretty ordinary looking."

"Ben, I know people in high places who can see that this doesn't happen."

The boy wiped at his tears. "Are you sure my dad will be safe?"

"I can guarantee it. I'm going to tell you a secret but this has to stay between the two of us. Promise?"

Ben nodded and Ray knew he would never share what he was about to tell him.

"Ben, not everyone knows that I do more than guide fishermen. . . ."

"I know," said Ben. "You dig graves for St. Mary's Church, too. I saw you when we were there for my mom's burial."

"Yes," said Ray with a chuckle, "I do that, too. But I'm also one of Sheriff Ferris's deputies when she needs someone who is good at tracking—whether that's people or vehicles or animals. I can help her find things. Right now, in fact, two people are missing over near Rhinelander and I need to get over there to help out. But what I want you to know is this. . . ."

Ray leaned forward to look Ben in the eye as he said, "I need to help Sheriff Ferris find the people behind this cheating that is happening in the fishing tournaments, too. This is serious stuff, Ben. These people belong in prison. Threatening your dad's research like that? That guy is w-a-a-y out of line. I'm not being funny when I say I want to see that jerk in jail."

Ben's eyes had widened as Ray spoke. "But I don't know his name. As far as I know, I've never seen him before."

"Not to worry. But I think he will show up again. He may think you're an easy target because you're a little younger than the other boys on the team." *And maybe because you don't have a mom*, Ray thought but did not say.

"Well, I'm sure as heck *not* an easy target," said the boy with such vehemence Ray felt compelled to give him a reassuring pat on the shoulder. "Tell me how I can help you and the sheriff and we'll do this, okay?" Ben went on. "Can I tell my dad about this?"

"Yes. I'll talk to him, too. We have to be careful, Ben. People involved in gambling can be dangerous."

"What do you want me to do?"

"You have a cell phone, right?"

Ben nodded.

"You've got my cell number. Text or call me when you spot this guy again. You don't need to engage the guy, but take note of any details you can see or hear. If you think he sees you or if he tries to talk to you, but send me the letter B for your name and where you're at. I'll know it's you and why. I'll take it from there."

"That's too easy."

Ray shrugged. "It isn't—we don't want him to know you're signaling anyone so be very careful. Be sure you're in a safe place when you text or call me." And just maybe, Ray thought, he should ask the other boys if anyone had approached them—or just warn them all about the possibility of someone offering bribes.

CHAPTER

5

THIRTY MINUTES LATER Ray pulled up next to Lew's cruiser, which was parked in the driveway of Ray's childhood home in Loon Lake. The family still owned the home, but Ray's father had retired and the couple had moved into a condo down in Madison for the winter.

"Thank goodness," said Lew, "we really need your help. Still no sign of the couple."

"Did you hear the one about the dyslexic guy who walked into a bra—"

"This is *not* the time for tasteless jokes," said Lew, trying to sound peeved while she was, in fact, relieved: the Ray she knew was back. And with that she filled Ray in on what the state troopers and the couple's son had shared.

* * *

"John and Miriam McKenzie have been members of the Wolf Watchers for three years and joined two other couples in setting up camps and watching stations up in Door County. But then the McKenzies decided to leave the group and go out on their own. They own property near Crandon and that's where the search is focused," said Lew, "But I know that you know more about the wildlife in this region than anyone, Ray. Would it be likely that they may have decided to head in this direction to find wolves to observe?"

"Could be," said Ray. "They didn't tell their son where they were going?"

"He travels a lot for work and said he hadn't been around recently to talk it over with them. He did know that his parents wanted some distance from the other couples and seemed to have split from the group for whatever reason. So he assumed they would head toward their summer home on Lake Lucerne, although he said his dad had mentioned the area around the Starks potato fields a couple times. And one of their friends told the troopers that the McKenzies knew there are six wolf packs in McBride County," said Lew. She smiled at him. "Which is why I thought of you."

* * *

Lew and Ray had a unique relationship. Though Ray had a history of misdemeanors due to his indulgence in weed before it became more socially acceptable (and less criminal), Lew was aware that his appearance and demeanor being at odds with the standards and rules of law enforcement could work for both of them. Ray's questionable behavior and free-and-easy lifestyle made it easy for him to get along with the bad actors who lived down roads with no street numbers for fire departments (hence hidden away from authorities), and his intuitive knowledge of the outdoors and his unrivaled skill at tracking humans and animals had made him indispensable as a sheriff's deputy.

The early morning coffee crowd at McDonald's could be relied upon to tout Ray's unusual talents: "That man tells the most inappropriate jokes—don't repeat them to your wife—but he can track a snake across a rock." It helped, too, that the crowd knew how he had come by his uncanny instincts for the waters and woods and creatures inhabiting the Northwoods.

As a seventh grader, booted out of St. Mary's School for two weeks for hiding a jar of live leeches in the desk of a girl he liked, Ray used that two weeks to change his life. He rode his bike to the nearby Ojibwa reservation, befriended two of the elders who let him pal along when they went fishing and listened carefully to every word they spoke.

They showed him how to track a bear, a wolf, a bobcat, a chipmunk—whether moving through the forest or among the sumac crowding the creek bed. They taught him to listen to the sounds carried on the wind and identify what those sounds could mean: a loon in distress? A great horned owl exulting after ripping the head off a rabbit?

Despite Ray's father being a physician, and his brother becoming a surgeon and his sister a litigator, after his two weeks with the Ojibwa elders, Ray had no appetite for a formal education. Those two weeks gave him everything he needed to live and learn from the most fascinating inhabitants of the Northwoods.

So it was that straight out of high school, he started a small business focused on . . . leeches. "I know leeches," he bragged, referring to the bait prized by many fishermen. Soon he was spending hours in the streams where he—illegally, of course—captured the wily creatures, then sold them privately until he had enough cash to open his own bait shop. The bait shop with its slogan of "Romance, Laughter, and Live Bait—Get It Here"—drew clients from all over Wisconsin, Michigan, and Minnesota.

Soon Ray was featured on TV shows highlighting his expertise with muskies and walleyes. A successful blog followed, plus a best-selling guidebook. Now, when not hired as a fishing guide by the enthusiasts who could afford him, he entertains his fans with his podcast that he called *Romance, Laughter, and Live Bait with Ray.*

* * *

"I have a hunch," said Ray as they lingered in the driveway of his childhood home. "Those of us who grew up in this neighborhood learned early on of a wolf den that was not far away. I'm sure it is still there and another one or two as well. We may be close to downtown Loon Lake but the swamp protects this area.

"I'm sure people like the Wolf Watchers are familiar with locations like this even though they prefer to set up their watching stations as far out as possible. They love the 'wilderness' aspect—much more romantic, dontcha know." He grimaced.

Surprised to hear that a wolf den could be so close to where they were parked, Lew looked around. She knew that Ray's family home was one of a half dozen large houses built in the 1950s on what was literally an island in the midst of a swamp (politely referred to as "wetlands" by real estate agents) located less than a mile from downtown Loon Lake. Given the risk of flooding in the spring, Lew had wondered why the area was so prized by Loon Lake's well-to-do. It was, she had learned after she joined the police force, a price the homeowners were willing to pay not only for their privacy but for the stately hemlocks and ancient white pines that guarded the island. "Lovely and hidden" described the large lots that had been sold.

"Lew, I wouldn't be surprised if the McKenzies had planned to set up a viewing site in the Robideaux Forest," said Ray, referring to an area less than a mile away from where they were. "That's what I would do. A natural area for wolves. I haven't been there in a few years but I hung out around there when I was a kid. I remember some old guys, loggers from Finland, built a log cabin way back in woods. I know there were wolves back in there then. The streams running through there and the surrounding forest made it a natural for wolf dens. There's a meadow that someone tried to farm once but there were too many rocks. That would make for a perfect site for watching wolves."

"Do you think the Wolf Watchers are familiar with the area?" asked Lew.

"If they aren't, they should be. You say this couple wanted to set up their own site for viewing?"

"Yes."

"Well, if they had a summer home in Crandon and were outdoorsy, then they would be familiar with the Robideaux Forest. The land was originally owned by a guy from Minneapolis who made millions in the logging industry in the late 1800s. He protected his land so it was never logged and it's still home to hemlocks and white pines you can rarely find these days. Years ago, his heirs gifted the land to Loon Lake, so it's been protected since."

"I assume they got a nice tax benefit?" Lew's tone was dry.

"No doubt, but today it's public land and some sections are popular with hunters from Milwaukee and Madison. If the state troopers haven't searched that area, we should start there."

Lew agreed, then made a quick call to the state trooper in charge of the search. She listened and then looked at Ray with a nod. "He's hoping we're right as they've had no luck yet," she said. "No sign of them. I'll follow you."

As she drove behind Ray, Lew had another thought and called the state trooper back. "Are you sure the McKenzies haven't left Wisconsin?" she asked. "They could be on the way to Yellowstone, which is famous for its Wolf Watchers."

"Good question," said the trooper. "I've been wondering the same. But here's something new to consider—I just learned that Dr. McKenzie didn't just randomly decide to move to another site. He had quite the confrontation with another member of their wolf-watching club. Not just an argument either. He destroyed some of the man's wolf-watching equipment—expensive long-distance telescopes and audio recorders—and came close to punching him out. We've been considering whether or not McKenzie may have decided to lay low since the man with whom he fought may have good reason to file charges for assault and property destruction. Or, if for those reasons, he may have chosen to leave the state. We know he's retired and has plenty of money so he can pretty much do whatever he wants."

Lew took this in. "So none of the wolf watchers they were originally with would know where they went?"

"Not a chance," the trooper replied. "The party whose equipment was smashed says they left in a hurry."

He paused for a moment, perhaps wondering how much to tell Lew, and went on. "We did question the man whose property was damaged quite closely as we did not rule out the possibility that in a rage he might have hurt the McKenzies himself."

"That sounds extreme," said Lew.

"I agree, Sheriff," said the state trooper, "but when you've worked with people dealing with anger and other serious issues for as long as I have—thirty-one years—you don't rule anything out. That's the big reason we are still searching the Door County area very, very carefully."

CHAPTER

6

"WE'LL GO IN from my folks' backyard," said Ray motioning for Lew to follow him around to the back of the house. "That's how I went in as a kid. Those days I wasn't interested in wolves—I wanted to spy on the old Finns," he said with a laugh, referring to the loggers who used to use the camp and who had come from Finland. "Boy, were those the days—no worries."

He opened a creaky wooden gate in the fence surrounding the backyard and they stepped into a heavily wooded area. Like a good hunting dog sniffing its way toward prey, Ray followed a path that was invisible to Lew. "Childhood memory," she told herself as they pushed forward.

* * *

Lew was no stranger to a childhood spent outdoors in the Northwoods. After her parents' early deaths in a car accident when she was seven years old, she had lived with her grandfather, who ran a sporting goods store in Tomahawk, not far from Loon Lake. He was a dedicated hunter and fisherman and he was the person who had introduced her to his passion: fly fishing. It was her own familiarity with the outdoors that prompted her admiration for Ray's skill. Among all the people she knew who could find their way through forests and over water, his instincts were the most remarkable.

The ground underfoot was firm but she could hear sounds from nearby streams. "Are we going to end up in the swamp?" she asked after they had been walking a good twenty minutes.

"No, we're on a peninsula with swamp on both sides. That's why it's still so beautiful, Sheriff. Over the years it has been impossible to develop this area. It isn't just protected by the wetlands but someone told me once that an underground river runs under all this. Our buddies, the wolves, are lucky sons of bitches, right?"

"I'd say so. These trees are magnificent." Lew paused to look around at the majestic hemlocks towering overhead while catching her breath. "Remember, Mr. Pradt, I'm fifty-two to your thirty-one—I need a short break here."

She decided to check in with Marlaine on the switchboard to be sure she had no alerts from the state troopers.

Nothing. Apparently no sign of the missing couple yet.

* * *

Cell phone put away, Lew followed Ray through the brush and into a small open meadow.

They trudged across the field, which was strewn with the rocks that had been left by the glaciers. As they neared the edge and a bank of sumac guarding the forest, Ray put a hand out to stop Lew. "Hold on, Sheriff. I see something odd . . . a metal roof . . . I think. Now what the heck? Let's go slow."

"What?" asked Lew, "what are you talking about?"

"The old loggers' cabin is right behind those pines. The last time I saw it, the little place was falling apart. On one end the roof was gone and. . . ." He had stopped talking as he moved ahead slowly. They were almost past a stand of balsam when Ray put his hand out again. "Stop. This is too damn weird. Someone has rebuilt that cabin."

"Maybe someone has turned it into a fancy cottage?"

"Off water? Give me a break. Also, isn't this public land?"

"Correct," said Lew, happy to be reminded they weren't trespassing.

As Ray kept his hand out to caution both of them, they crept through the trees and up to the small cabin. From where she was standing, Lew could see it had a porch running along one side and two windows on the back.

Before they moved further, Ray paused to take a long look around them.

"What?" asked Lew, "you look worried."

"Not worried—mystified. That road leading up to the cabin is new. And well used. Fact is, when I was a kid there wasn't a road in here, just paths and a logging lane. Even then, you had to know where you were going. Let me take a look out front, see if someone is here."

Lew waited as Ray hurried to the front of the cabin, then returned. "No one in sight. Let's check this out." Peering through the windows at the back of the cabin, they could make out wooden crates stacked in piles across the room.

"Interesting," said Lew under her breath. Her law enforcement instincts were on high alert.

"Let's see if the door is unlocked," said Ray, heading back to the front of the cabin. To their surprise it was. "I imagine whoever owns this place is coming and going so often, they aren't too worried about theft. . . ."

"Plus it's in the middle of nowhere," said Lew.

"Hidden by trees," said Ray, his tone grim.

One box was open and Lew peered in. She whistled. "You won't believe this." Ray leaned to look over her shoulder. "An Uzi," said Lew, "that is one illegal gun. Jeez, an Uzi is a machine gun."

"Check this out," said Ray ten seconds later. "AR-15s, half a dozen of the damn things. Sheriff, these are lethal weapons. They shoot dozens, if not hundreds, of bullets at once. Bullets that don't just kill people, they go through anything in their way."

"You're telling me?" Lew stood up straight. "I don't need to see more. Bet you all the boxes are packed with guns. We're gonna lock this place down."

With that they stepped back outside while Lew put out an alert for two deputies to join them. She started to give directions to the cabin from the main entrance to the Robideaux Forest when she paused to ask, "Do you think the way here is marked? I don't see anything on my GPS."

"Let's go back to your cruiser and give it a try," said Ray.

As they hurried across the meadow and through the forest, Lew said, "By the way, before I forget, do you mind telling me what your problem was when I called you earlier?"

"Sure, it's nothing I can't handle. Has to do with the boys I'm coaching for the fishing tournament. Some creep leaned on one of the kids and scared the bejesus out of him—trying to enlist him to cheat."

"Cheat? How?"

"Fake his catch early in the tournament so the jokers betting on it have an advantage."

Lew frowned. "That's as illegal as those damn guns," she said. "It's a major issue for law enforcement right now, too. I was just at a seminar on how prevalent cheating is in sports gambling, not to mention gambling on fishing tournaments is illegal in Wisconsin—always has been and not likely to change."

"Not surprised," said Ray.

"Tell me more. Did the kid give you a name? He might be on our watch list."

"No. He was so terrified by the guy and his threats that he ran away from home . . . but only for a few hours."

"Ran away? Why on earth—"

"He was afraid that his participating in the tournament and refusing to cheat would cause the people behind the cheating to hurt his father. The jerk who leaned on him threatened him and said they could yank the money for the grants that fund his dad's work. He ran thinking he could protect his dad somehow. Crazy, I know, but the kid is barely sixteen. He's young and worries too easily. His mom died last year so I'm sure he's grieving, and that doesn't help, Lew."

Lew noticed that Ray used her name as opposed to calling her "Sheriff," which meant he was more worried about the incident than he was letting on.

"Who is this young man?" asked Lew, growing worried herself. Ray's story had jarred a memory of her own son's death in a bar fight when he was just seventeen.

"He's the star of my tournament team—Ben Mason. His dad is a professor at the University, Robert Mason."

"I know Rob—he's a fly fishing buddy of mine."

* * *

The sudden memory of the death of her son, Chris, had caught Lew off-guard. She had divorced his father, whom she had married fresh out of high school. Denny had been a charismatic teenager—handsome, easygoing, athletic. Only after she married him did Lew discover he was lazy and an alcoholic. The few times she described him to people later, she said "he was one of those guys who thought they could wear their letter jacket and be number one forever."

The hard part after the divorce was her ex's continuing influence over their son, the older of their two children. Lew had gone to work as a secretary at the paper mill and put the children in day care only to find that Denny would—without asking—pick up their son and take him to the bars with him.

Lew fought Denny in court but lost. He won custody of their son as soon as the boy turned ten. Again, Denny was able to charm the judge and get his way. The boy slipped into his father's ways and soon ended up hanging with a crowd of young toughs. It was after a fight with another boy who knocked out one of Chris's front teeth that she met Dr. Paul Osborne, the dentist who replaced his tooth and charged her very little.

* * *

Little did she know that fifteen years later, after the death of his wife, that not only would she and Dr. Paul Osborne come to know each other as "Lew" and "Doc," but they would trade nights cooking and washing dishes at one another's homes—either his lake house or her farm. Friendly evenings that led to quiet nights together.

But that was years after the bar fight when Chris's crowd got into it with a gang of boys from nearby Tomahawk, the awful night when Chris was shot and killed. A night when a distraught and heartbroken Lew wanted to shoot and kill her ex-husband, Denny, who had led the boy down a bad path and who she held responsible for the boy's death.

Instead she joined law enforcement. She was fortunate in her timing, as women were just being welcomed into law enforcement. Her years of hunting with her grandfather and helping in his sporting goods store had given her solid experience with guns of all types and sizes. She was not just skilled with various rifles and handguns but she was strong and well muscled, able to work long hours, to carry heavy loads, and to defend herself. She was as prepared for the challenges of law enforcement as any man applying for the same position. And when the man who had hired her retired, who did he recommend to replace him: Lewellyn Ferris. Her only regret was that her grandfather was not alive to see her promoted to Loon Lake Chief of Police.

Strangely enough, it was during one of her early years on the Loon Lake Police Department that she pulled over an inebriated driver whom she recognized: Dr. Paul Osborne. He was still reeling from the unexpected death of his wife of thirty years. He may not have loved his wife, who was a serial complainer dedicated to furniture, clothes, and bridge games but she had provided a structure to his days. When she was gone, he found himself alone, lost and floundering, and turned to drinking.

The arrest turned out to be a gift to him and his family. His two daughters used it as the trigger for an intervention that led to Osborne's spending time at the Hazelden/Betty Ford Drug and Alcohol Treatment Center.

"You know you saved my life," he said to Lew when they connected in a trout stream a few months after he had returned home from Hazelden. Now that his wife, who had hated his muskie fishing and the money spent on it, was no longer alive, he was able to pursue another fishing sport he had always admired: fly fishing for trout.

The local instructor recommended by *Ralph's Sporting Goods*? A person who moonlighted from her day job as a cop? That was one Lewellyn Ferris.

CHAPTER 7

ONCE THEY MADE it back to the road running alongside the forest, Lew backed up and turned around to drive toward the municipal entrance to the hiking paths.

"Wait, stop," said Ray in a loud voice as she was rounding a curve. "Back up, please. Not far, maybe a hundred feet or so. I think I saw something." Hearing the urgency in his voice, Lew followed his instructions.

They had passed a tiny abandoned red brick building with a faded wooden sign over broken front steps that read TOWN HALL. "Back up another twenty, thirty feet," said Ray.

Lew checked her side mirror and did as she was told. Studying the roadside, she could see what appeared to be a barely discernible two-lane dirt road running alongside the ancient town hall and disappearing behind it. She didn't need instructions from Ray to turn in. Soon they found themselves making a sharp turn behind the building after which the road continued on into the Robideaux Forest.

"Interesting . . . you can barely see this entrance from that town road," said Lew as they bumped along. In less than ten minutes, they pulled up in front of the old loggers' cabin. No other vehicles appeared to have arrived since they'd left. Not only was the clearing in front of the cabin wide enough to accommodate three or four vehicles, but off to one side was an outhouse, looking as ancient as the cabin.

"An outhouse!" said Ray. "Bet that place has some cobwebs."

Lew reached for her cell and placed calls to two deputies. After giving directions and describing the contents of the wooden crates, she instructed them to treat the area as a crime scene. "We'll need this location watched day and night until I can arrest whoever it is that's hiding these dangerous weapons." With that, she assigned each to eight-hour surveillance shifts.

She then checked in with Marlaine on the switchboard and alerted her and the rest of her staff to the situation, saying, "Any calls from one of our men on watch, be sure to see if they need backup and—night or day—alert me ASAP."

"There's no sign of that missing couple," said Ray when she was off the phone. He had taken a short walk around the clearing where they were parked, "but I did see that more than one vehicle has driven back here. Worth checking out unless you hear those people have been found."

"Don't hesitate, please," said Lew. "If I did not say so earlier, you are officially deputized to assist with this search. Since I haven't had any news from the state troopers, I figure the search is still on."

"Can't do it at the moment," said Ray with a dismissive wave of his hand, "I have a meeting with my tournament high school fishing team in half an hour but it shouldn't take long. I can be back out here within two hours."

"Something is going on here that's for sure," said Lew, "likely unconnected to the missing couple, the McKenzies, but what we just saw is alarming. *Submachine* guns? AR-15s? What the hell? Somebody's gunrunning, and looking at prison for this operation." She glanced at Ray. "Okay, I'll run you back to your pickup as soon as one of my deputies shows up."

Less than five minutes later, Deputy Phil Craig was climbing out of his squad car. After alerting the deputy to the contents of the cabin and the need to arrest anyone driving up who might be involved with the guns, she added, "I'll also make a call down to the Wausau Crime Lab as they should be able to get prints off the guns and maybe off some surfaces or items in the cabin or the outhouse."

* * *

Back in her office, Lew met with her IT wizard, Dani Wright. "I need everything you can get me on the Robideaux Forest," she said. "History, background, owners, the works."

"Will do," said Dani, turning in her desk chair to contemplate the large screen in front of her. After typing in Robideaux Forest, her fingers sped across the keys. Forty-five minutes later she handed Lew a three-page printout.

"The Forest was the favorite hunting ground of a man named Louis Olsson who was one of the early pulp mill owners in the logging heydays of the eighteen eighties when sandstone grinders were used. He sold out in the early nineteen hundreds but kept one piece of property for his own private hunting land. It was land he refused to let loggers clear-cut like they did the rest of the Northwoods.

"Louis had one son, Oscar, who inherited everything, including the forest. Oscar, who ended up living in Lake Forest, Illinois, was no hunter and decided to gift the forest to Loon Lake for recreational use—but to allow no hunting. He has two grandsons, Eric and Andy. Andy and their father, Grant, challenged Oscar Olsson's will in hopes of regaining ownership of the Forest but the State Supreme Court refused to hear their lawsuit. Robideaux Forest belongs to the town of Loon Lake, period."

"Any mention of people living in the Forest over the years?" asked Lew. "Like even decades ago?"

"No. Not a word—only that it is a beautiful recreation area and only bike and walking trails are allowed to be built. No buildings. That old Town Hall you mentioned? That is not on Forest land but on county land that abuts the Forest."

"So there are Olssons still around the area? What do we know about them?"

"I have their names and my search shows them living in the Chicago area—in Lake Forest to be exact. The father is Grant Olsson and his adult sons are Eric and Andy. That's all I can find."

"It's a start," said Lew. "Thanks, Dani."

After the meeting with Dani, Lew called Ray. No answer. "Hmm, his meeting with his tournament team must be running late," she thought. After dealing with several calls and emails that had come in while she was gone, she checked with the state trooper handling the search for the McKenzie couple.

"Nothing, sorry to say, Sheriff," he said, sounding frustrated, "we've found no trace yet. We did think we had found something once we learned about that serious altercation up in Door County between Dr. McKenzie and another one of the Wolf Watchers. What we learned was how angry McKenzie was simply because another man had intruded on what he thought was his viewing area—these wolf watchers can be pretty territorial, it seems—and in a fit of anger he destroyed the guy's very expensive equipment."

"Yes, you mentioned that when we talked earlier. Any update?"

"We followed up on that, in case the man whose equipment was destroyed and trip was ruined perhaps retaliated in some way, but, fortunately, we were wrong. The man whose equipment was destroyed had returned to his home in Milwaukee right away, and neighbors verified that. He says he refused to deal with McKenzie—certainly not confront him."

"Did the man file a police report?" Lew asked.

"No, at least not yet. He did say he might have to file a report to get insurance to cover his loss, or he might decide just to let it go, although almost certainly the McKenzies would have been asked to leave the wolf-watching group."

"Anything else useful?"

"Only that other than his temper, McKenzie 'has a 'bossy' side to him . . . I wonder if Dr. McKenzie 'bossed' the wrong guy, y'know? Otherwise, all I can tell you is the family is very worried. Anything on your end? Though I know there's no indication they might have headed your way. . . ."

"Sorry. Nothing yet but I have a deputy checking out an area where we know there's long been sightings of at least one pack of wolves. On the off chance that that information may have caught the McKenzies' attention, he's going to check it out. And when I say, 'check it out,' he will give the area a very careful going over. Ray Pradt is my deputy's name and he's known for his tracking skills. If there is even a hint of anything to be found, I'm confident Ray will find it."

"Thank you, Sheriff, this is a difficult situation."

"I can only imagine," said Lew in sympathy. "That poor family."

Off the phone, she packed up her laptop and headed out to Osborne's. It was Doc's night to cook dinner.

CHAPTER

8

AFTER PARKING, LEW let herself into the back room where Osborne kept all his outdoor gear and fishing poles. She stopped as she often did to enjoy looking at a framed photo on the wall to her right. It hung just below his favorite musky rods and featured three people: Osborne in his fishing khakis standing beside his daughters, Mallory and Erin. The daughters were eleven and nine years old at the time, and the youngest, Erin, standing on the outside, held a stringer from which hung a forty-six inch musky—her first. Her father was beaming. As were both girls.

Lew found it an iconic photo for a couple of reasons. First, while both girls had inherited their father's lanky physique—tall and slim—they didn't look alike otherwise. Mallory, the elder, was dark-haired and olive-skinned with dark eyes like her father, who had inherited his Metis coloring from his Ojibwa great grandmother.

Erin, on the other hand, looked like her late mother, Mary Lee, who had been fair-skinned with light blond hair.

For Lew the photo underscored the futility of Doc's late wife's Mary Lee's hatred of her husband's devotion to the outdoors. *Too bad she couldn't have enjoyed the outdoors along with her husband and daughters—or at least not tried to block their enjoyment.* Apparently she had frequently voiced her disgust with fishing, saying: "Those fish are smelly and I hate the taste. Can't you give it up and golf, for heaven's sake?"

It seemed that Mary Lee had charmed Osborne when he was fresh out of dental school. He had spent his teens in an all-boys Jesuit boarding school, and his mother had died when he was six. His father had never remarried, so Osborne grew up in an all-male household, leaving him susceptible to female charms.

But it was no secret that Mary Lee, who had pursued him with soft smiles and adoring eyes in her early twenties, changed after their daughters were born. It turned out what she had really wanted in a husband was a man who made the kind of money that would buy a "lovely home," nice clothes, and an impressive car. A man her bridge partners would covet. She did not bargain for a fisherman or daughters who also loved the outdoors. Worse yet, she didn't need "crummy small-town Loon Lake."

Her constant complaint was: "Why can't we move to Milwaukee, Paul? You know you can earn double the money with a city practice." Osborne had found himself stuck. But having grown up without a harmonious marriage to observe, plus being aware that other men he knew had grumpy wives—and being devoted to his daughters—Osborne had put up with Mary Lee for thirty long and mutually unhappy years.

The photo of Doc and his daughters tended to remind Lew how different she was from the other women in Doc's life. For one thing, she was not tall and slim. Lew, who was eleven years younger than Osborne's sixty-three years, was five feet seven inches in height and had never been svelte. While she would describe her wide, firm shoulders and hips as "stocky," Osborne would disagree, insisting "The right word to describe you, Lewellyn, is stalwart—stalwart and beautiful." That left her feeling abashed but happy.

She was also quite different from the late Mary Lee as she did not want Doc to "just keep quiet" after dinner. She loved their evening chats and, even more, the humor they shared. If she was asked to characterize the life they shared—three nights at his lake home and three nights at her small farmhouse with each person cooking and doing the dishes at their own place—she would have to say they enjoyed "a close friendship." And even though Doc insisted on asking her to marry him, she would only grin, punch him in the shoulder and say, "Hell, no, why ruin a good thing?!"

Neither of them had had good marriages.

* * *

As she was standing in front of the photo of Osborne and his daughters and mulling over her good fortune,

Osborne poked his head through the door from the kitchen to say, "If you don't hurry, my perfect mashed potatoes and roast chicken will have to be fed to that raccoon hiding behind the garage. . . ."

"Sorry, sorry," said Lew, laughing as she set her Sig Sauer nine millimeter gun on the shelf reserved for it and followed him to the kitchen table. "Ooh, that looks delicious and I am starving, Doc," she said as she sat down.

After inhaling the mashed potatoes and gravy right away, she asked, "What do you know about the Robideaux Forest, Doc? Was it public property when you were a kid? Or still owned by the Robideaux family?"

"I knew it well," said Osborne as he tackled a chicken thigh, "my dad's house was a block from the upper section of the forest. A couple of my friends and I used to explore those woods all the time. We loved spying on the old loggers." As he chewed away, Lew's mouth dropped open.

"Serious? You know about that old cabin?"

"Cabin? C'mon, that was a shack. Stuck way back in there like a haunted house. Yeah, whenever I was home from boarding school, my buddies and I, there were three of us, we'd hunker down, crawl through the brush and keep going straight until we came to the little stream that ran alongside the old place. We called it 'The Finns,' after the Finnish loggers who used it." He chuckled. "All we ever did was hide and watch.

"We could see five or six old guys walking around, probably picking up sticks for their firepit. I think they were loggers and that's where they slept. By the time I was twelve, they were gone and the old place falling apart. Another friend and I went inside once but all we found was some old wooden racks where they must have slept. Even the firepit was outside. God knows how they made it through the winter."

"Did you ever talk to them?"

"No, oh no, we were too scared. Lew, we were eight, nine years old at the time. At one time we actually thought they were ghosts."

"And Robideaux? Did you know the family?"

"The old man, who made a fortune with his pulp mills, was barely alive when I was young, though my dad treated him for something. At least that's all I remember. Dad was a dentist, too, remember. I think there were only two dentists in Loon Lake back in those days, so anyone with a toothache was likely to see my dad or Dr. Metternich.

"After old Robideaux died, leaving an enormous fortune—he'd put his money into the first bank, the first railroad, the first phone company—hell, the first *everything* in Loon Lake, so his two children inherited quite a fortune. One son died young, I think pneumonia or something, and the daughter, who married a guy named Oscar Olsson, inherited it all."

"And she lived in Loon Lake?"

"No, she died in her late forties and her husband who grew up in Lake Forest inherited her estate. He used to come north pretty often. I met him once but he's long gone. His son, Grant, has to be in his late eighties. It was Oscar who gifted the land to the town. He was quite the wheeler-dealer, and he knew he could get a nice tax break on that. He didn't hunt or fish so he didn't mind giving it up.

"You know, Lew, if you need to know more about Grant Olsson, you should come have coffee with me and my buddies at McDonald's. A couple guys are old enough to have done business with that razzbonya. They can bend your ear."

"Does that mean he's not the kindest, gentlest soul?"

"You betcha. Grant took to promoting himself as a financial advisor and bilked a few folks out of a lot of money. But he's got smart lawyers, and they got his case moved to Pike County where he paid off the judge. Yep, old Grant got away with it but no one in McBride County will even talk to the guy anymore."

"Sounds like Robideaux Forest is the only good thing that family has done?"

Doc shrugged. "Who knows? I may be overstating his bad behaviors, but he doesn't have many friends around here. Legend has it old Robideaux was not the kindest either."

"Tell me again where you went in to find the old shack, because that's what Ray and I found this afternoon. It's been restored and someone is using it as a hiding place for illegal guns like Uzis and AR-15 semi-automatics. We know there's no easy access to it these days and I've got it under surveillance, so whoever thinks they have a great hiding place is about to get a big surprise."

Lew suddenly thought of something. "That reminds me," she said, getting up from the table, "excuse me a minute, Doc."

"Better hurry," said Osborne, "I've got rhubarb pie."

Lew hurried through the living room to the porch where she peered through the side window. "I'm checking to see if Ray is home yet," she called back over her shoulder. "He was meeting with the fishing tournament team and was supposed to meet up with me . . . but I don't see his truck." Disappointed, Lew returned to the kitchen. "He sent me a text that he 'learned something' about the Robideaux Forest. With no news on the missing couple, I'm wondering what he learned. But no sign of the guy, darn it."

Having finished her chicken while she was talking, she picked up her fork to tackle the pie that Osborne had set before her, she said, "Gosh, this is delicious, Doc. Thank you."

The proximity of Ray's trailer home, painted to look from the front like a neon-green leaping musky, had a been a near deal-breaker in Osborne's marriage to Mary Lee. After they had purchased the land for their planned lake home, she had discovered that "that disgusting Ray Pradt" had put a house trailer in plain sight of their front windows, and she began legal proceedings to have him evicted from land he had bought legally. Though plantings of young balsam trees promised to partially obscure his trailer, she was adamant: "That man has to go, Paul. You have got to make him move that awful, awful trailer."

Then fate intervened. One snowy night Mary Lee's bronchial infection turned suddenly worse. Osborne knew she needed immediate care from the emergency doctors at St. Mary's Hospital but the raging blizzard caused his car to get stuck in their driveway. A desperate call to Ray, who had four-wheel drive on the pickup he used for snow-plowing, led to Ray ("that disgusting fishing idiot") rushing Osborne and Mary Lee to the emergency room. Mary Lee didn't survive, but Ray's courageous attempt to rescue her initiated a friendship between himself and Osborne. It was a friendship furthered when, months later, they discovered they were both attending the meetings held behind the door with the coffee pot on the glazed window: Alcoholics Anonymous.

While Ray had worked his way into heavy drinking in his early twenties, only to be shaped up at age thirty by a woman determined to marry him who insisted he go to AA—the meetings were a success, but not the relationship—Osborne's slide into a disastrous pattern occurred after Mary Lee's death. She may have harangued and ignored him but she had structured and controlled his life for thirty years, and he felt some guilt over her passing. Should he have given up fishing? Should he had insisted more stringently that she go to the doctor earlier? When she was gone, his world seemed empty. His daughters were grown and gone, living their own adult lives and he had retired from his busy dental practice.

Acute loneliness haunted him. With beer, wine, and whiskey, he tried to fill the void until the day he was pulled over and given a DUI by Loon Lake Police Officer Lewellyn Ferris, and his daughters held an intervention. Months at the Hazelden Betty Ford Drug and Alcohol Treatment Center stabilized him. That and the day he walked into his first Loon Lake AA meeting where, to his surprise, he found an empty chair next to a familiar face: his next-door neighbor! It was a moment that changed his life. And Ray's, too. They were good for each other.

* * *

Frustrated by seeing no signs of life in Ray's trailer windows, Lew was about to give up when she spotted his pickup parked in the clearing in front of his trailer. *At least he was back.* The brass leaping walleye decorating the pickup's hood gleamed in the light from the setting sun. "Back in a minute, Doc," she said as she ran for Osborne's back door, across his yard, down the rutted two-lane drive to Ray's and, without knocking, burst through the mouth of the neon green musky.

"I got your text message, Ray. What's up?" asked Lew, raising her voice to a shout before she saw Ray, standing nearby at his kitchen counter. Looking over at his visitor, he gave a wave encouraging her to calm down as he finished pouring a can of soda.

"Found out I graduated with the woman who's the director of the Robideaux Forest. I'm meeting with her at eight tomorrow morning and thought you might like to be there."

Lew tried to hide her disappointment, "Sure, that should work."

"No, Sheriff," said Ray, seeing the look on her face, "this is not wasting time. Sharon told me that even though they maintain strict access to the Robideaux Forest, letting people use only designated roads and trails, there are utility roads that may make it easier for me to search the areas where the wolf dens are known to be located."

"Ray, I seriously doubt the McKenzies would have gone that far off the public trail system. They're middle-aged people who follow the rules. . . ."

"In theory, but remember that Dr. McKenzie got so irate while wolf watching that he trashed another member's equipment, actually a criminal offense—that's not rule following, and it's clear he has a temper," said Ray. "And I gotta tell ya, once I saw that meadow behind the cabin, I'm convinced the McKenzies may have spotted it from a distance and planned to use it for a wolf-watching site there. . . ."

"You think they're hiding back in the woods?" Lew gave a rueful laugh.

"I think they may have lost their way looking for that site. Or, okay, have run into the people smuggling weapons and gotten into trouble. Worth a try, don't you think?"

"Since I have not heard a word from the state troopers . . . ," she paused, thinking. "Heck, it's a long shot, but let's do it. I know Dani tried to bring the area up on Google Maps but with all those old hemlocks and white pines, she couldn't see past the cover.

"On another note, Ray, how's young Ben? If he hears from anyone affiliated with the gambling crowd again, I want to know. I talked to the team investigating the gambling operations and they want to identify who approached young Ben."

"Right now Ben seems fine," said Ray, "and, no, not a word from that guy who threatened him. Ben's a quiet kid, so it's hard to tell what he's thinking. A great team leader. You know, Sheriff, I think my boys have a good shot at winning the tournament. All we need is one big fish—one *giant* fish," Ray grinned.

* * *

Though it was after ten when Lew and Doc snuggled down under the comforter on his bed, she found it hard to fall asleep. She waited to hear his soft snore, then got up and moved to the open window. The September breeze carried an edge, alerting the great horned owl it was time to prepare for snow. The lake was calm, its silver surface a soft shimmer under the moon.

Yet all she could think of was the bad news sure to arrive at any moment: a man and woman, missed by their family, found lying somewhere in dense woods—alone. Dense woods where it is too quiet and only wolves are watching.

CHAPTER 9

Eight o'clock Wednesday morning found Lew and Ray in Lew's cruiser waiting outside the small building that held the Robideaux Forest director's office. On discovering that the door was locked, Lew had returned to the car disappointed.

"She said eight this morning?" she asked Ray, as much to make the time pass as to confirm their appointment. Before Ray could answer, a red SUV drove up.

Ray jumped from the passenger seat and ran over to help the driver, a petite blond woman, as she got out of her car.

"Sharon Warner, Ray Pradt," Lew heard him say, "I'd like you to meet someone but, first, weren't you and I in the same English class senior year?"

"We sure were," said the woman, "and, Ray, I'll never forget those really bad jokes you told in Mr. Fisher's class. . . ."

"Yeah," said Ray with a sheepish grin, "I got an F one semester. Learned my lesson—"

"No, he didn't," said Lew, interrupting the two as she walked over to join them. "He tells worse jokes these days."

To underscore his determination to continue his nonconforming behavior, Ray waited for Sharon to unlock her office door, then, before entering after the two women, he let go with a loud loon call. Sharon, delighted, gave him a hearty punch on the shoulder. Watching the two enjoy each other, Lew hoped the woman was in a long and happy marriage. Otherwise, she could see Ray on his way to breaking yet another woman's heart.

After Sharon got the coffee maker brewing, the three of them sat down at her desk.

"I'll start," said Lew, "but, first, I have to ask you to keep the information I'm about to share confidential as I have an investigation underway and do not want any news reaching the public."

"I understand, Sheriff Ferris," said Sharon, "not to worry. Everything we discuss will remain confidential unless you specify there are things you need me to share with my staff."

Lew started by telling Sharon about the missing couple and the hope she and Ray had that they may have driven to the forest with plans to set up a wolf-watcher site. "We have no reason to think this other than Ray and I are aware we have six wolf packs here in McBride County and that the male of the couple was upset that someone else was watching in what he considered his territory."

"No doubt there are wolves here," said Sharon. "I haven't seen any myself but several of my colleagues have. I'll touch base with them and get some locations for you."

"But a new development we stumbled on yesterday," said Lew, "is that you have someone using that old cabin way back behind the abandoned Town Hall to buy and sell illegal firearms. . . ."

"Oh my God," said Sharon, leaping to her feet. "Let me call the police right now."

Putting a hand on her arm, Lew urged Sharon to sit down, saying, "I *am* the police. And I already have the cabin under surveillance by my deputies. So just know that we need to prevent the general public from getting anywhere close to that location. Are there any other ways in to that area that need to be blocked off?"

"Not that I'm aware of," said Sharon. "We'll check the utility roads but there is only one that goes anywhere near there other than the road you've blocked." She paused as if to reflect. "Wow. I wonder how long the gunrunning has been going on. I feel like I've let our community down. . . ."

"Don't beat yourself up until we know more," said Lew. "There's a reason criminals get away with serious crime like this: they know how to hide."

That didn't help. Sharon was obviously upset.

* * *

Sharon Warner had eyes and demeanor so serious, Lew knew she could trust her. After describing in more detail what she and Ray had found at the cabin and the reason for the presence of the McBride County deputies at the location, Lew said, "I need to know any and all access points to that area, including by foot or all-terrain vehicle."

"And how to reach that meadow that's behind the stand of balsams," said Ray. "Is there a trail that allows the general public to find their way in there?"

"Yes and no," said Sharon, unfolding one of several hand-drawn maps. "This is a sketch of the utility roads we've been building to help the forest research teams who are studying wildlife in the Robideaux Forest. The roads have been off-limits to the public but several are due to be opened for use shortly."

With a slight smile, she added, "This is my special project. Before I took this job, no one had paid much attention to the Robideaux Forest, which is one of the few virgin forests left in Wisconsin."

"That may explain why someone has been able to come and go from the old logger place," said Ray.

"Afraid so, but I'm determined to see that that doesn't happen again. So, look," she said as she turned one of the maps so Lew and Ray could see it more easily. "Here is a sketch of the utility roads that we've built to run back into the different sections. We won't allow the general public on all those roads. Most are old logging lanes and could be dangerous for some folks. But I will give you both passes today to allow full access.

Also, the map will be sent to a print shop shortly so it will be much clearer and easy to use.

"Sheriff Ferris, how many passes for the utility roads do you need for your deputies?" she asked, pulling open one of the desk drawers.

* * *

Satisfied with their meeting and pleased that the Robideaux Forest director was so cooperative, Lew and Ray took their leave. As they drove back to her offices, Ray studied one of the two maps Sharon had copied for them. The utility roads were sketched in sharply enough that Ray could make out the various locations where vehicles could enter.

"I like one of these," he said, pointing to one road on the map as Lew pulled into her parking spot. "It looks like it runs along one edge of that meadow. If it's okay with you, Sheriff, I'd like to run out there later this morning. I have no clients today, and the tournament team doesn't need me until tomorrow. Not likely to find anything we haven't seen already but sure worth a good look."

"I agree," said Lew. "I'm in meetings this afternoon and I have a call in to the FBI to report the illegal firearms, but let me know if you see anything. And if I hear from the state troopers, I'll send a text. Oh, and when you see young Ben again, tell him I'd like to take him and his dad fly fishing, will you? If he's good with muskies, he may enjoy a fly rod."

"I'll bet he's fly fished with his old man," said Ray, climbing out of the cruiser. "Probably *fly fished* for muskie."

* * *

Forty-five minutes later, Ray called on Lew's personal cell. His voice was somber. "Sad news, Sheriff. I found them—their bodies, that is. Get out here now. I'm on that utility road we had decided on when I left you."

"First, I have to call the state trooper running the case. Can you give me a location?"

"No, do not call the trooper, Lew. I need you to wait until I show you what I've found. Please, trust me. Just get out here ASAP." There was no lightness in his voice, and she knew to take him seriously.

She heard him take a deep breath before he said, "We don't want to risk too many feet on the ground until you and I have cordoned off the area and I haven't been able to check all of it yet. So all I'm asking is for you to take twenty minutes to get here and twenty for me to show you what I see. *Then* you call. We have to be sure we mark all entry points 'cause there may have been more than one person executing—"

Lew broke in. "Yes, I hear you, but I am calling Bruce at the Wausau Crime Lab. You know it will take him at least an hour to get here."

"He should use the helicopter. We need him and his people as soon as possible."

Lew clicked off her phone and looked at the two police chiefs with whom she had been meeting. "Sorry, guys, a big emergency. I'll update you shortly but this isn't in your jurisdictions, at least not at the moment."

Two minutes later, she was out of the building and pulling her cruiser onto the county highway.

CHAPTER

10

THE UTILITY ROAD that she and Ray had decided was the closest to the wolf meadow was just past the main entrance to the Robideaux Forest and hidden behind a large storage building. As the dirt lane curved around the building, Lew could make out the path, overgrown but wide enough for a car or small truck. She drove ahead but after she had driven close to a mile on the grass and rocks, she wondered if she had chosen the right one. At that moment she caught sight of Ray's pickup parked off to one side.

Good. Ray had to be close. Pulling into the narrow lane behind the pickup, she decided to worry about backing out later. As she got out of her cruiser, she heard Ray call, "Here, Sheriff Ferris, over this way . . . can you hear me?"

Twenty steps past the pickup, she found Ray standing beside a white Toyota SUV.

Dreading the answer, she asked, "Are the McKenzies in the car?"

"No." Ray gestured for her to follow him.

"No?" she asked, finding his answer troubling. *What on earth?* She followed as he moved deeper into the woods along another path, one hidden from all but the eyes of deer—and one who seemed to think and move like them, Ray Pradt.

Lew figured the almost invisible path had to be a vestige of the logging days in the late 1800s. What the loggers had left, generations of deer had been using to travel through the stands of hemlock, white pine, and balsam. As Ray pushed forward up an incline, Lew was relieved that the day was clear, not rainy or threatening an early, slippery snow.

It was ten minutes before Ray stopped and waited for her to catch up. When she did, he pointed ahead, beckoning for her to move around him. She squeezed through the low-growing branches crowding the path. At first all she saw was a large hole carved out of the ground to one side of the path, the soil black and fresh. She stepped closer, eyes scanning an area that appeared to have been dug up.

"Possums," said Ray, answering her unasked question, "until the eagle scared 'em away."

The bodies lay face down where they appeared to have been buried before the wildlife took over. The effect was unsettling and Lew gave her stomach a moment to relax. She glanced at Ray.

"Don't move another inch, Lew," he said as he reached for her right arm to keep her from moving forward.

"I thought it wise for you to see this before the family comes and before the Wausau Crime Lab takes over. Bruce's forensic experts can confirm time of death, I know, but there may be a hint or two here that you and I might recognize, a hint of who may have done this. . . ."

"Like the people hiding those guns?"

"Exactly. Who else would have known about this location?"

"How did the McKenzies know?"

"My hunch, and I'll share this with Bruce along with other signs of the movements here, is that the McKenzies stumbled on the old logging cabin when whoever was hiding the guns happened to be there and was caught by surprise. I think you and I discovered the old cabin not long after they had been killed there and the bodies moved here."

Lew surveyed the area. "What made you decide to look here?" she asked her friend, taking a deep breath.

"Hard to see it from where we're standing right now but we're just fifty feet from one side of the meadow where the wolf dens are likely located. When I started out this morning, my plan was to check the perimeter of that meadow first because I figured the meadow is what might have drawn the McKenzies to this area.

"Having seen tire tracks parked in the clearing at the old cabin, I followed one set that crossed the meadow and that is where I found the SUV. From there I followed another set of tire tracks that soon stopped and turned around. Just past where that vehicle had turned around, I saw the footprints of an individual that continued further into the woods. Also, the footprints are deep enough that I suspect the person walking was carrying a load, likely the body of one of the McKenzies. Assuming he wasn't too bright, my bet is the guy who did this planned for critters to take care of the victims. He sure as hell didn't bury them very deep."

Glancing around him as he spoke, Ray said, "This is far enough into the Robideaux Forest that it's likely not even the victims' bones would ever have been found. What the perpetrator didn't know is that he was hiding the McKenzie's SUV right where Sharon's crew planned to restore an old logging lane and turn it into a utility road. That's my bet."

As he spoke, Lew shivered. "Why do I feel like we're not alone, Ray?"

"We aren't. The wolves are watching."

CHAPTER

11

"I HAVE TO CALL Bruce Peters again before I do anything else," said Lew as they made their way back to where the McKenzie SUV was parked. She glanced in it—completely empty, from what she could see: no bags, no wolf-watching equipment. "When I tried him earlier, his assistant said he was finishing a report on a murder case that was due in court within the hour and he'd get back to me right after that. But he hasn't called so I need to try him again."

She grimaced. "Once I reach him, I gotta call the state troopers. The victims' son is with them and less than an hour from here. I know he'll be grief-stricken and want to rush over here. Knowing that, I'll feel so much better if I'm able to get Bruce and his forensic team from the Wausau Crime Lab here first to protect the scene. Sorry for thinking out loud, Ray."

"Not to worry," said Ray. "But I just had another thought. Before anyone besides you and me gets here, I'd like to go back and walk the perimeter of the area where the bodies are in case I see another point of access. Likely not, but I feel like whoever did this may not have paid attention to the tracks they'd left coming and going."

"People never do," said Lew, "that's why I put up with you and your weed habit."

"C'mon, Sheriff, I haven't smoked a joint in over a year now." Before Lew could say anything, he said without a smile, "I'm damn sure whoever killed this poor, unsuspecting couple left something behind and I need to find it. Bruce's guys are good but not as good as me."

"If you can find *it,* I can find *them*," said Lew finishing his thought while punching in Bruce Peters's cell number. "I need them to check the old logging cabin and that outhouse for prints, too. Who knows how many people are behind this."

A moment later, Bruce answered her call.

"Yo, Sheriff," said a deep voice loud and happy as always, "sorry I missed your call earlier. How did you know I've been dreaming about a Blue Winged Olive hatch? Are you calling to persuade me to join you in the Prairie River this evening?"

Lew managed a grim chuckle. "Not sure about that, Bruce. Maybe tomorrow night at the earliest. I'm calling because I have a disturbing crime scene up here and I need your forensic expertise," she paused, then gave her good friend a break saying, "that is, an expert who has learned to carry just six dry flies at a time."

Bruce hooted. In spite of communicating through fiber optic cables, Lew swore she could see his bushy black eyebrows bouncing up and down. "I'm the man. And, by the way, I've been stewing over my frustration with the double haul lately but, hey," his voice turned serious as he said, "enough of my baloney. What's up?"

"You may be aware the state troopers have been searching for an older couple from Milwaukee whose family reported them missing two days ago?"

"Yes, sounds like they were hiking and got lost over in the Crandon area east of Rhinelander?"

"That's the couple. Not hikers, wolf watchers, looking for a new site from which to watch the critters. And not lost, Bruce, at least not as of twenty minutes ago. Murdered. Ray Pradt just located the victims and their vehicle here in Loon Lake. Are you familiar with the Robideaux Forest?

"I'm aware of it. I've never been there but bringing it up on my screen as we speak. You've called at the right time, by the way. Just closed a case earlier this morning. How many of my people do you anticipate needing? Oh, and FYI, your best buddy, Doug Jesperson, is off at a seminar so I'm in charge. You won't have to bargain for manpower this time." Again, Lew could see Bruce grin through the phone lines.

"That is good news," said Lew, relieved. Jesperson was the titular head of the Wausau Crime Lab, though

Bruce and several of his colleagues handled the day-to day-investigations.

* * *

More critical, from Lew's perspective, was the fact that Jesperson, even as he was nearing retirement, was still as biased against women in law enforcement as he had been twenty years earlier when she had joined the Loon Lake Police Department. A bias he never hid and that prompted him to make remarks that should have already gotten him sued. Lew would never forget how he greeted her the first time she had to work one on one with him and his "Wausau boys" as the crime lab crews were called at the time. This was shortly after she had been promoted to chief of the Loon Lake Police Department.

"What are you doing here, girl?" were his first words that day, followed by a dismissive look and, "Is your big boss on his way?"

"I'm the big boss," Lew had said. "I'm the new Chief of the Loon Lake Police. Chief Lewellyn Ferris, Mr. Jesperson, glad to meet you and I look forward to working with you." She had held out her hand, which he had brushed away as he stomped off. That was the friendliest he ever got.

It was also why she was happy to take Bruce Peters on as one of her flyfishing students. The friendship they developed made it easy for her to find work-arounds when she needed the forensic talents of the Wausau Crime Lab.

Today she and Bruce could "barter" their time: "I'll trade you two hours of learning to double haul on the

Prairie River for autopsies on two murder victims." It wasn't meant to be disrespectful to the victims, but was a way to get the job done and done well, and not let the absolute grimness of the job get them down. They could have a little chuckle, but get things done efficiently and well.

* * *

"How is the trout season up there these fall days?" asked Bruce. "I have a brand-new, expensive-as-hell fly rod. . . ."

"Bring it along," said Lew. She liked the sound of that. She found new state-of-the-art flyfishing equipment intriguing, and she enjoyed teaching Bruce, one of the most enthusiastic students she'd ever had. He was one of the reasons she continued to teach even though her responsibilities as McBride County Sheriff made it tough to find the time.

"Bruce, when I get off our call, I have to alert the state troopers running the search for the missing couple so I'm sure the victims' family members will be here within the hour. . . ."

"I can grab our copter,'" said Bruce. "Please keep them away from the victims until we—"

"Don't worry, Ray and I will have the entire area secured, but it would help to have you here as soon as possible."

* * *

Forty-five minutes later, as Lew and Ray were waiting in the office of the Robideaux Forest director, she watched as a dark blue SUV pulled into the small parking lot. A couple who appeared to be in their thirties scrambled out of the car and moved quickly toward the office. From the tense look on their faces, Lew knew they had to be members of the McKenzie family.

"Darn," thought Lew as they approached, "they got here too soon. Just ahead of Bruce Peters's arrival."

She stood as they entered. The man, whose face was twisted with grief, said, "Sheriff Ferris, I'm Brian McKenzie, the son of Dr. John McKenzie and Miriam—it's my parents who are missing. This is my wife, Riley. . . ." Lew saw a man in his thirties, tall and rangy, with light brown hair and dark brown eyes; the woman beside him was also tall and slender, and Lew sensed she was going to be a strong source of support for her husband.

"Yes, Mr. McKenzie," said Lew, shaking Brian McKenzie's hand, "we spoke briefly yesterday by phone. I'm Sheriff Ferris and this is Deputy Ray Pradt, one of my chief deputies and an expert tracker. It's Deputy Pradt who located your parents. We are so sorry for your loss and we're determined to find the people who did this. Right now, Brian, we're expecting the Wausau Crime Lab's forensic experts. They should arrive any moment." She checked her watch.

"Brian and Riley, once the forensic people are here, I'll be taking them to the area where we found your parents. Once again, I am so sorry to have to give you this news. . . ." She paused, unsure what to say next. Lew could see Brian, who appeared to be in his early thirties, struggling to keep his composure. His wife was holding a supportive arm around her husband's waist, her own face streaked with tears.

Hoping to make the waiting time pass, Lew asked the couple, "Have you been to this area before?"

"Yes," said Brian, "I'm a cross-country skier and skied a race here last winter."

"Don't forget to tell her you took scuba diving lessons over in Minocqua two summers ago," added Riley. "That's why Brian has so little hair," she said, trying hard to add a little humor to their tense wait. "He keeps it short for his scuba mask. So short his mom likes to kid Brian that he looks so young he'll get carded at a bar for not being twenty-one. So, yes, Sheriff, we know our way around here a little. . . ."

Before anyone could say more, a squad car pulled up and Bruce Peters jumped out. He rushed into the office where everyone was standing. "Sheriff Ferris, Deputy Pradt—sorry I couldn't get here sooner. The rest of my team will be here within the hour; they're driving up from Wausau."

With that Bruce turned away to look at the couple standing nearby. "Am I correct in assuming that you are the McKenzie family members?" He extended a hand to Brian and Riley as he said, "This has to be a difficult situation for you folks. No words for this. All I can say is do not hesitate to ask me any questions."

And with that he laid out how he and his forensic team would approach the sites where the car had been found and where the bodies were located. As he was speaking, two state troopers walked in and sat down to listen and take notes.

When Bruce had finished, Brian said, "Thank you, Mr. Peters. I appreciate you're taking the time to give us these details and I understand the importance of not interrupting your work. Just let us know when and if we can do anything to help out. We will be extremely careful not to damage or compromise any evidence, so don't hold back if we're risking that, please."

"Then you'll understand if I ask you to stay here at the director's office until we've completed our initial investigation," said Bruce.

"Of course," said Bruce with a nod. "How soon will I be able to see them?"

"Give me your cell phone number," said Bruce, "I'll call you from the site once I assess the situation."

* * *

Walking back to the area where Ray had found the bodies, Lew noticed for the first time how raw and trampled the earth was around the still forms. Pointing to small footprints in the soil, around the bodies, Ray said to Bruce, "I told Lew before that I'm sure those prints have been left by possums."

"You are absolutely right," said Bruce. "I don't think the family needs to see this. What's your opinion, Sheriff Ferris?"

"I agree and I'll talk to them. I'll stress the importance of allowing your forensic pathologist to study the remains as they are, *where* they are." She was quiet for a long moment, then said, "We do need official identifications though. Should I have Doc Osborne handle that before the bodies are moved?"

"Talk to him; see if he's okay with that and how soon he can get here," said Bruce. "I know he's an expert in forensic odontology."

"I'll call him now," said Lew. She knew that the sooner the victims could be identified, the sooner arrangements could be put in place to move the bodies down to the Wausau Crime Lab for autopsies. "I'm sure Doc will need dental records so I'll see if the family can help us with that."

CHAPTER

12

BACK AT HOME, Lew was trying to relax with Doc, but she couldn't get the two bodies out of her mind.

"Lewellyn, this is what forensic odontology is all about. Believe me, I've seen worse," said Osborne after Lew had described the damage she thought possums had been guilty of having wreaked on the bodies.

"Well, I sure haven't," said Lew. "My worry is that their son and his wife will want to view his parents before the autopsies. Given what the possums have done . . . I'm not sure how to prepare them. I know I wouldn't want to see my loved ones in that condition."

"Would you be comfortable letting me handle this?" asked Osborne in a gentle tone.

"I would love that," said Lew, relieved.

* * *

As always, she found Doc's suggestions wise, grounded in fact, and, frankly, calming. Once she had caught sight of the damage caused to the victims' bodies by the wildlife, she hadn't been sure how to alert the family. The gruesome sight could be so disturbing, it could cloud their memories and cause them to overlook or forget details that might help Lew and her deputies locate the people—or person—behind the devasting crime.

Ray's speculation that the McKenzies may have accidentally run into or interrupted whoever was storing the illegal guns in the renovated old cabin made sense. She would need to investigate that, but it was a good starting point. The first thing to do now was find who is trafficking in the guns. No small order.

As she mulled that over, she found it reassuring that Doc Osborne would be able to get the official identification of the victims underway, which would speed the investigation run by Bruce and the Wausau Crime Lab.

"Doc, do you think you'll be able to tell if they were shot?" she asked now.

"Not sure. You may need the crime lab's forensic pathologist for that. I'll tell you what I need right now as I'm driving in your direction is to please ask the McKenzies' son to have his parents' dentist forward their dental records to me ASAP."

"I'll call him now," said Lew. "And I will meet you at the director's office where the family is waiting. "I'll be there shortly myself. And, Doc, thank you again."

Ten minutes after Osborne and Brian McKenzie had spoken with the McKenzies' dentist, whom they were able to reach in his office, the dental records showed up in Osborne and Bruce Peter's email accounts. Relieved, Lew was about to leave the director's office when Brian's wife, Riley, spoke up. "Excuse me, Sheriff Ferris, do you know if anyone has found my mother-in-law's cell phone? There might be some information on that."

"I'm sure that's high on the investigators' list, Riley. I will double-check, though, to be sure," said Lew. While she was speaking, there was a knock on the door and in walked Bruce's forensic colleagues, two men and a woman. ("So much for everyone calling them 'the Wausau boys,'" thought Lew at the sight of the young woman.) After introductions, Lew directed them toward the utility road and, with Doc following in his car, drove ahead to show everyone the way.

* * *

It was seven thirty that evening when Bruce called Lew to say, "You were right—no fishing tonight. But I do have interesting news. We've searched the McKenzies' car, which had been stripped of everything, including personal effects—even the glove compartment was emptied. I'm sending the vehicle down to our lab for a complete analysis, as it has plenty of fingerprints, but the question will be whether or not any of those prints belong to the person or persons who executed the McKenzies—"

"Wait," said Lew, "what do you mean 'executed'?"

"Thought you might find that interesting," said Bruce. "Did you know that Ray was able to locate the spot where they were killed?"

"No, once I got your colleagues and Doc out to the site, I've been in the office all afternoon. Thought it best to stay out of everyone's way. What do we know now?"

"The couple appears to have found that old logging lane, the one that runs behind the town hall building—the same one you and Ray found and that's been used by people coming and going from that old cabin. We think the couple pulled into the clearing in front of the old logging cabin while someone was inside. I'm sure they walked up to the door, friendly as anything, only to surprise the hell out of your gun trafficker. We know it was at least one person, maybe two, who walked the couple back out the door and off into the woods. At gunpoint, I'm sure. Now this is my theory, Sheriff. We have yet to prove anything."

He took a breath and then went on. "Whoever it was shot them both in the back of the head, execution style. It appears the bodies were then wrapped in a tarp and transported in the perpetrator's vehicle—likely the bed of a pickup—to where they were found. The couple's SUV was moved later. If you can find the van or truck the perpetrator used, it's highly likely we can get blood samples to prove they were involved."

"So, no blood in the SUV?"

"No, though we may find prints."

"And why are the bodies in such terrible condition? It wasn't possums did all that, was it?" asked Lew.

"No, not possums though they did some damage. The weapon used on those poor folks is what did the damage. Now, Sheriff Ferris, we'll be working this until dark and likely finish up by midday tomorrow. Thanks to your pal, Ray, we've been able to find what's left of their cell phones, the wife's purse, and her husband's wallet. The phones were smashed and everything thrown back into the woods but we found most of it. We'll keep searching.

"Two of my team members are heading back down to Wausau now to get more analysis done on the items, plus submit some DNA samples and prints found in the cabin to several national law enforcement databases, which may help us identify who these people are. Two of us will stay overnight. I've checked us in to the Loon Lake Inn, which, fortunately, had openings."

"Have you updated the McKenzies' son and his wife?" asked Lew.

"Not yet. I thought you might want to handle that."

"And Doc Osborne, is he with you folks out there at the site?"

"Yes. He said he'll be calling you shortly. Thanks to his expertise, I have the two IDs confirmed and I'll be able to have the victims moved down to our crime lab shortly. The ambulance is on its way."

* * *

Off the phone, Lew sat back in her chair, thinking. Her personal cell phone rang and she heard Osborne's voice.

"Yes, Doc, I just got the details from Bruce. I'm about to leave the office and head out to the director's office to meet with the family. See you there?"

"Yes," said Osborne, "and I will walk them through what I learned and what they might consider moving forward."

CHAPTER 13

TWENTY MINUTES LATER, Lew walked into the director's office behind Osborne.

"Brian, you look exhausted," said Osborne. "I suggest you let me talk with the folks at the funeral home you'll be using. I've worked with cases like this before and I can answer any questions they may have."

"Thank you, Dr. Osborne," said Brian. "Given what you've told me about the condition of my parents' bodies, I think it wise we arrange for cremation as soon as they are released from the Wausau Crime Lab. Does that make sense?"

"Yes, indeed," said Osborne. "I know this isn't easy but I'll share with you my own experience, which may help a little."

"You've had family shot in the head?" asked Brian, not sarcastically but apparently in earnest.

"No. But I was six years old when I was told my mother had died after a long illness. My father knew that she had lost so much weight and it had been so long since I had seen her because she had been in treatment at the Mayo Clinic that I might find the sight of her too shocking. He wanted me to remember my mother the last time she held me. . . ." Osborne paused and Lew saw tears welling in his eyes. She could only imagine what that memory must be in his heart.

"So . . . my father arranged for her cremation and he put in front of the urn that held her ashes a picture of my mother and myself sitting together. It had been taken on my birthday. In that photo my mother looked so lovely and I looked so happy. As sad as that day was, my memory is of my mother holding me and loving me."

"That's what I want for my mom and dad," said Brian. Then he turned and wept into his wife's shoulder. Watching him—tall and fit, athletic with a robust history of cross-country skiing and scuba diving—Lew couldn't help seeing past the handsome man with the dark brown eyes to the sad young boy who had lost the two people who had held him close to their hearts. She knew his devastation even as she knew there was little anyone could do to help him in his grief.

A few minutes later, after Lew had given Brian and Riley the news about the belongings found and the fact that the cell phones had been destroyed, Riley asked, "Did they find Miriam's AirPods?"

"Not sure," said Lew.

"They're so small and Miriam tended to keep them in a pocket of whatever she was wearing, like maybe her slacks or her jacket. I know it's a long shot but sometimes you can track people with those just like you can use smart phones. Call me crazy, but I'm willing to try anything in case the person who killed my in-laws may have taken them by accident."

"This is good to know," said Lew. "Hold on, I'm going to call Bruce right now before they move their bodies. Something small like that—we don't want it to drop out, get lost."

Walking into the other room while Osborne continued to talk with Brian and Riley, Lew alerted Bruce to watch for the AirPods. "Hold on," he said, "the ambulance crew is here now. Let me check. . . ." She didn't have to wait more than a minute or two before he was back on the line. "No, no sign of them. That's good news. Because maybe we can put a trace on them, but to do that we'll need access to the name and password locking the cell phone. Please check to see if there's any chance the family might have that information."

Lew delivered the news to Brian and Riley. Even as Brian shook his head sadly, saying "No," his wife, Riley, spoke up. "I may be able to get that information," she said. "Miriam told me that she and John had recently updated their wills and she made sure to put copies in their safe deposit box along with a list of all their devices and passwords. My mother-in-law was a very careful person. If the bank will give Brian access to their safe deposit box, which he should, since Miriam made sure that Brian has power of attorney, so we may be able to get her password for the iPhone and AirPods."

"It's too late for me to call the bank now," said Brian, "but I'll call and try to meet with them first thing tomorrow."

"As soon as possible," said Lew. "I have an expert IT person on my staff and she may be able to help us. If there's anything to be found, she can do it."

CHAPTER

14

THE THUNDERSTORM HIT shortly after nine that night. Officer Reed Maron squinted through the intense downpour with little luck. Driving on the outskirts of Loon Lake, he passed two cars that had pulled over, their emergency lights flashing. As he rounded the corner into the downtown area, a semitrailer passed, throwing up a shower of water that totally obscured his vision. "This is not smart," he said to himself, "better take a five-minute break until this storm blows over."

He pulled into the closest parking spot, which was in front of the scuzzy Woodpecker Bar. Hurrying out of his squad car, the officer ran to duck through the front door of the bar, justifying his entrance into the joint as a good way to spot potential DUIs. The little place was crowded, which he suspected it always was by this time of night. Sliding onto a stool at the end of the bar, he ordered a nonalcoholic beer and listened to the crashing of the thunder, which was easy to hear through the flimsy walls of the old place. Right after he was served, two men ducked in, soaking wet, and took the barstools next to him. No sooner had they sat down than a flash of lightning took out the dim lighting in the bar.

It was so dark that Officer Maron could barely make out the faces of the men sitting nearby. They must have had the same problem as they didn't appear to notice his uniform. At least that's what he assumed when their conversation turned to a subject they might not have wanted to have overheard by a law enforcement officer.

"Yeah, last month I made forty-five hundred," said the man sitting right beside the deputy. "How did you do?"

"Hell, I made twelve grand. I had an AK-47—just what the old man and his son wanted. Wish I had that this week. Of course, helps they take deliveries only on Fridays. Gives me a couple more days to see what I can scrounge up. Helps, too, they got our drop-off back in the Robideaux Forest, dontcha know."

"Least they could do since they make us wait while they take forever to check the guns out. But twelve grand, you lucky dog! Wish I could find an AK-47. Sold 'em a ghost gun they loved a couple weeks ago but that got me just five grand. I gotta do better finding stuff on line."

"Hey, don't forget the ol' AR-15s—everybody wants those and Grant and Andy give good money for 'em. They can move those suckers in a second."

The men were quiet for a moment. Then the one seated closest to Reed asked his buddy, "Where do you find that many AR-15s? Online?"

"Hell, no, Bert. I check out the trunks of SUVs and trucks parked in front of bars—bars like this one, y'know. And the beds of pickups. Same joints. Guys don't think to lock up when they stop for a quick beer. So I wait until after ten or ten-thirty, then start at one end of town and work my way up. Only got caught once and told the cop I'd had one too many and climbed into the wrong vehicle. . . ."

"And he believed you?"

"If he didn't, he didn't say nothing. But my best sources are down in Milwaukee. Some of those dudes get stuff coming in from outside the States, y'know. Can't believe how many Uzis are out there."

With those words, Officer Maron decided not to push his luck. He swung away from the two men and set his feet silently on the linoleum tiles, hoping they wouldn't notice him leaving. Out the door, he ducked into the rain, which was letting up, pulled out his phone and shot photos of the license plates of the three pickups that he knew had pulled over after him. He hoped he got the ones belonging to the men in the bar.

Once in his own vehicle, he called his chief at home to report what he had just heard.

"Call Sheriff Ferris right now," said Loon Lake Police Chief Todd Donovan, "this is what she is working on. She needs to hear this ASAP."

* * *

The call from Officer Reed Maron had wakened Lew but not Osborne. She managed to crawl out of bed without disturbing the man who was sleeping soundly beside her. She crept into the living room, closing the bedroom door behind her and finished the conversation with the officer with a warm thank-you: "This is a lucky break, Officer Maron. You can't believe how important this is. Thank the Lord for the heavy rainfall—"

"And scuzzy bars," said Maron. "Please know I don't make a habit of patronizing that joint. . . ."

"I believe you. But thank goodness you did tonight."

"Should I be calling for backup and bring these two in tonight?"

Lew thought for a moment. "No. We'll try to identify them, and let me work this tomorrow, as I think they may lead us to the people running the operation. That's who we need."

Off her cell phone, she walked over to gaze out the big picture window to where the moon was busy silvering the lake. Though Osborne might have unpleasant memories of his late wife's insistence on building a big, expensive lake house, he was willing to concede that her insistence on this remarkable view had been fortuitous. The vision below through one ancient white pine, its long, graceful needles framing the moon's delicate efforts was soothing. That quiet beauty paired with the news that could help solve a difficult case made Lew feel better about going back to bed. And so she did.

CHAPTER

15

EARLY THURSDAY MORNING, Ben Mason was second in line when Ralph's Sporting Goods opened. Muskie reel in hand, he was hoping to find that Ralph's had plenty of the fishing line he needed. Seeing that Ralph, the owner, was busy with his first customer, Ben wandered down the aisle where all the fishing lines were on display. He was mulling over two different ones when he heard a pleasant voice with a familiar tone say, "Hey there, Mr. Mason, are you ready for the big day Saturday?"

Ben swung around. He was stunned to see a tall man with a balding hairline and dark brown eyes. The face held a friendly expression but the man looked so much like the one who had tried to get him to cheat during the walleye tournament that he had to be the same guy. Ben panicked. Mumbling and nodding, he backed away and hurried down the aisle to the back of the store where he knew the store had an unmarked men's room. Once inside, he grabbed his cell phone and hit Ray Pradt's number.

"He's here," said Ben in a harsh whisper. "That man is here, Mr. Pradt!"

"Who? Where? Ben, are you okay?" asked Ray.

"I'm at Ralph's and that man is here," said Ben, sputtering a little. "He talked to me but I took off. I'm fine. I'm hiding out in the men's room." He sounded upset, but not panicky.

"Good timing, you caught me having breakfast at the Pub, Ben. I'll be right there," said Ray.

And he was. Less than five minutes later, Ben heard a soft knock on the men's room door and heard Ray's voice calling his name. He cracked the door open far enough to see Ray waving for him to come out.

"Take it easy, Ben," said Ray in a low voice as they walked back into the store toward the counter where Ralph was checking out a customer. "Act natural, like we're out shopping. Just show me the guy if he's still here."

As they neared the aisle where Ben had been looking at fishing line, he stopped and pointed. "But . . . maybe I'm wrong," the teenager said. The man he had seen was still there but now Ben wasn't so sure he was the same one who had terrified him the first time. "He looks kinda like that guy, but now, well, I'm not so sure," Ben said in a whisper to Ray. "The other guy had, well, more hair."

At that moment, the man glanced over at the two of them and said, "Hi, sorry if I startled you, young man.

I just wanted to say how much I enjoy seeing you and your team hold up your winning muskies. Saw you in the tournament up in Boulder last month. Those are nice fish you guys catch."

Ray stepped forward and, holding out his right hand, said, "Hello, there, we've met before. I'm Ray Pradt. Didn't I guide you and your brother once?"

"Years ago," said the man, shaking Ray's hand in return, "I'm Eric and you took me and Andy out on Lake Wisnocki but that was a good ten years ago. Good memory."

"What's your brother up to these days? He's not the guy running the sports betting operation, is he?" asked Ray.

"Oh, yeah," said Eric. "He did okay with NASCAR and thinks he can do fishing tournaments, too."

"Ah," said Ray, smiling grimly as he spoke. "Give him a message for me, will you?"

"Sure, you looking for new clients?"

"No, not that. Just tell him to stay away from the high school and college fishing tournaments. These are young guys, they're just learning how to be expert fishermen and they don't need to have sports betting dirty the water, pardon my expression. And—in case your brother's too stupid to notice—gambling on fishing tournaments is illegal in Wisconsin. Now and—if I have anything to do with it—forever."

Taken aback by Ray's vehemence, Eric Olsson stammered saying, "Is Andy violating the law? I can't imagine. . . ."

"Could be it's a rumor he's as involved as it sounds like, but you can tell him I said it's a bad idea. Keep his mitts off the high school and college kids and stick with the walleye tournaments in the states where betting on fishing tournaments is allowed. There's plenty of old guys to bet on in those tournaments."

Looking puzzled but still friendly, Eric raised a hand. "Will do, Pradt. I'll definitely pass that along." He looked over at Ben and said, "Good luck this weekend, young man. I'll hope to see you up on the podium." Then he walked off in the direction of the store entrance.

After making sure Eric had left the building, Ray motioned for Ben to follow him to see Ralph. He pulled the owner aside, saying, "Can Ben and I have a minute with you, Ralph?"

"You sure can," said the store owner. "Need something custom for this young expert here?"

"No, but we need some answers. Ben, here, thought he was pressured to do something he didn't want to do by someone who looks a lot like Eric Olsson. Could it have been his brother by chance? I know this sounds crazy but. . . ."

"Nope. Those two could almost be identical twins even though they're a couple years apart," said Ralph. "I get 'em mixed up myself and I've known the Olsson family for years. These days Eric's hair is thinning so it's easier to know who's who even though they got the same coloring. But Andy's got another twenty pounds on him and he dresses like a biker. Eric? He dresses like what he is: a banker." Ralph grinned at his little joke.

Then he went on. "But it's funny, you're asking, Ray. Andy was in just the other day wanting my opinion on some of the guys fishing the walleye tournament down south in Illinois next week. Said he's running a sports betting start-up and doing his research. Funny guy, Andy. You know, those two guys may be brothers and look a little alike but, boy, are they different."

"How so?" asked Ray.

"Well, that one, Eric, reminds me of his mom. She passed a couple years ago but what a nice woman. Kind, funny. She did her Christmas shopping here. She always said, 'Ralph, my men are hunters and fishermen—all they want is sports stuff.' And, boy, did she spend money on 'sports stuff.'" Ralph chuckled.

"So Eric reminds you of Evelyn, huh?" said Ray.

"Yep, but Andy's like his old man—has that sort of dark edge. You know, Grant inherited a bloody fortune and lost it all in the stock market, the dot-com crash years ago."

"No, I didn't know that."

"Yep, but he's back in the money these days. The family trust came through with a stake in the Rhinelander paper mill. Nothing like what he had before but enough to set him up to deal in antique guns. He's got a nice business going now except for one thing," said Ralph, tipping his head and raising his eyebrows signaling something private.

"Oh, yeah?" Ray knew that Ralph knew he could keep a secret.

Leaning forward and making sure no one was nearby, Ralph continued in a low tone. "He keeps trying to unload crap for me to sell on consignment—used and damaged AR-15s—that kind of thing. Told him and that son of his that I got a reputation to keep." Ralph dropped his voice to a whisper. "I am not taking stolen goods. Bottom line. Y'know, sometimes I think the old man has dementia. He has to know I'm the last guy he should approach with that junk."

"Got it," said Ray. "Thanks, Ralph. This is a big help."

"Hope so," said Ralph with a wink at Ben. "Good luck Saturday, kid. I'm pulling for you."

* * *

Lew pulled into the clearing in front of the old logging cabin and parked next to an unmarked car she knew belonged to one of her deputies. She had assigned four sheriff's deputies to keep the cabin under surveillance on a rotating schedule. When she got the message from Loon Lake Police Officer Reed Maron, the lack of visitors, much less sightings of suspicious cars now made sense: the cabin was being used by the gun traffickers on Fridays only. If she was lucky, tomorrow would be a big day. The guys moving guns wouldn't know she had the old place under surveillance until it was too late. The thought made her happy.

Before the deputy on duty could open the door for her, a battered pickup with a leaping walleye on the hood pulled up to park next to her cruiser. Ray Pradt, of course.

"Ray, I wasn't expecting you—what's up?" asked Lew before reminding herself that welcoming Ray with a question could be hazardous.

"Well, just had coffee with a guy who's addicted to brake fluid. . . ."

Trying hard to keep her patience under control, Lew waited. Again, she reminded herself that Ray's torture usually preceded good news. "Oh, yeah?" was all she said.

"Yep, he says he can stop any time."

"Lame," said Lew. "Got anything better?"

Ray got slowly, very slowly, out of his pickup. He was sporting a wide-brimmed straw hat topped with a stuffed walleye whose head and tail extended, as he said, east and west, above his ears. A handsewn gift from a former girlfriend, Ray had a habit of wearing this treasure when he was feeling especially good.

Once out of his pickup, Ray leaned back against the truck, pushed his walleye back on his head, crossed his arms and said, "Got a strong lead on who's running the guns here."

Lew stared at him. "For real?

"Pretty sure. Looks like it could be one of the Olsson boys and their old man. Andy, the younger one, is the same jerk who tried to scare young Ben Mason into helping him fix our fishing tournament."

With that he shared what Ralph had told him about how the two Olssons, father and son, were allegedly dealing in antique guns and also how they tried to off-load damaged or less expensive current models on Ralph. “And they wanted him to pay them for the crappy merch,” said Ray. “Sounds to me like they might be the guys moving the guns through here.”

“You may be right,” said Lew and shared what Officer Reed Maron had overheard at the bar. When she was done, Ray whistled. “Looks like we got a busy Friday, Sheriff.”

“Yes, and a dangerous one,” said Lew. “Question is: Will Grant Olsson and his son cooperate?”

“Or head for Canada?”

“Right. And who is bringing them the illegal guns? I’d like to nail their suppliers too.”

“You need help,” said Ray.

“A lot of help,” said Lew. “The good news is the FBI is sending people. I’m expecting them any time. One of the guys coming is a good friend of Bruce’s.”

“A fly fisherman?”

“Maybe. Could be me, Bruce, and his buddy in the Prairie River tonight. Want to join us?” Lew grinned. She knew fly fishing could never replace Ray’s love for muskie and walleye fishing.

“Nope. Last night of working with the boys getting ready for the tournament this week,” said Ray. As he was talking, Lew’s cell phone rang. She looked down at an unfamiliar number.

“Yes?” she asked, hoping she hadn’t entered the spam universe.

“Sheriff Ferris, this is Riley McKenzie. I have some interesting news if you have a moment.”

"Certainly," said Lew, stepping aside and remembering that she had given Brian and his wife Riley her personal cell number.

"I went through my mother-in-law's files last night and found a copy of the passwords that she had put in their safe deposit box. So I have her iPhone password and it should work for her AirPods. Did Mr. Peters and his investigators find the AirPods?"

"I don't know," said Lew, "but I'll double-check as I'll be talking to Bruce shortly.

"What makes you think the AirPods may be important?"

"If the person who killed my in-laws and smashed their phones took the AirPods, then they can be traced. I can use the "Find My Phone" app and it may show us the location of the AirPods."

"Hmm," said Lew. "May be a long shot. Do you think the killers would have kept her AirPods?" Lew herself had never used the devices.

"I understand. But I also know that people who are hooked on iPhones tend to use the AirPods, too. Not everyone is aware that they give off signals. I see it every day. I think I told you I teach English in our middle school where we're seeing kids who lose AirPods, use their iPhones to find them. I'm sure Miriam would have had hers hanging around her neck or in one of her pockets when she and John were driving around the area. She was never without the darn things."

This sounded significant. "Good work, Riley. I'll run this by Bruce ASAP and let you know if they've been found or are missing."

"Thank you, Sheriff. I know it's a long shot—"

"My IT expert thinks like you do, Riley, so we'll check this out. Long shots are long shots until they aren't. You never know."

C H A P T E R

16

Lew was just finishing her lunch when a smooth bald head and two dark eyes peered around her open door.

"Okay to interrupt?" asked the man, eyeing the half-eaten egg salad sandwich on her desk. "I'm Pete Cooke with the FBI, Bruce Peters's buddy. I think you're expecting me?"

"I am, I am, Pete. Please, come in," said Lew, managing to swallow one last bite of her sandwich before tossing her lunch remains into the wastebasket under her desk and scrambling to her feet. "Bruce has said good things about you. Guess you two have known each other a long time?"

"Yep. Grew up together outside Merrill where we both played on our high school basketball team. Bruce is one smart guy—he aced AP Chemistry while I switched to physics." Pete chuckled. "Oh, and he's a terrific fly fisherman."

"That's right," said Lew, "he mentioned that you fly fish. Am I correct?" she asked. As Pete settled into one of the chairs in front of her desk, she reached over to shake his hand.

"You don't grow up where we did in the heart of brookie country and not fly fish," he said, grinning.

Normally reserved when meeting new people, Lew couldn't help liking this guy right off the bat. Tall and sturdily built with an open face, she watched as he took in who she was: a woman, makeup free, of average height with broad shoulders and hips and a cap of unruly dark curls kept short and tucked out of the way. She liked what she saw in his eyes: humor and trust. That said it all. They would get along.

"Do you have a few minutes to tell me about the two victims? Bruce said they called themselves 'Wolf Watchers'?"

"Yes, they did and I'm more than happy to share what we know so far. I have a good half hour before my next meeting," said Lew. She gave a snort of exasperation. "For the record, Pete, it's times like this is when I'm frustrated being a sheriff—too much administrative stuff. Meetings, meetings, meetings. . . ."

"I know what you mean," said Pete, nodding. "That's why I like working in the field. So these Wolf Watchers. . . . I've heard the term before but I thought that was a group based out west in Yellowstone National Park. Didn't know they had members around here."

"The victims, the McKenzies, were a husband and wife who were among a small group organizing Wolf Watchers down in the Milwaukee area. Several couples, friends of theirs, had spent time with the folks in Yellowstone Park. Working with the people out west, they learned how to watch in teams using spotting scopes, which they would set up near one another so they could all watch the same pack.

"As I'm sure you know, wolves can be hard to see, especially when sleeping or moving through the dense evergreens and brush native to this region. Open areas, such as meadows, make seeing the packs easier, which is why the wolf watchers tend to all be so close to one another. They set up their wildlife viewing scopes and use radios to alert one another when they see a wolf or signs of a pack.

"What I understand from the McKenzies' son, Brian, is that Dr. McKenzie got frustrated always being around so many other watchers, which is why he and his wife set out to find another spot. But the truth is that Dr. McKenzie got into a big fight over his watch site, which led the state troopers to investigate if that altercation might have turned into something worse."

"I take it that wasn't the case?" asked Pete.

"No, thank goodness. But after leaving the group, Dr. McKenzie was determined to find a pack to watch or as he said to his son, 'our own pack.' And that's why the couple drove over here. We have six wolf packs in McBride County."

Pete whistled. "Whoa. Six? They must be everywhere. Sure it's safe to go fishing?"

Lew laughed. "Hey, you know wolves. They prey on the weak and you do not strike me as weak."

Now it was Pete's turn to laugh.

After they had both chortled for a moment, she got back to business.

"So the other day, it seems, the McKenzies were driving through an area here called the Robideaux Forest, which has never been logged. The forest is virgin timber with magnificent old hemlock and white pines and was donated to the town of Loon Lake years ago by the original owner, a man who had made a fortune in the logging industry and used the Robideaux Forest as his own private hunting ground.

"My theory is that when the McKenzies were driving on a back road, exploring the Robideaux Forest, they stumbled across an old logging cabin tucked back in the woods and that, unbeknownst to them—or to us—was being used by gun traffickers."

"So they surprised the wrong people."

Lew nodded. "You got it. Pete, I'm sure Bruce has shared with you the basics: that the McKenzies were murdered and their car hidden in the forest, as were their bodies. All their belongings have been stolen or were destroyed. We've found no trace of their wolf-watching equipment, winter clothing, computers, spotting scopes. . . . Nothing. All gone. Their phones were smashed so no tracing calls or texts, of course, and apparently no cloud backup."

"And guns?" asked Pete. "I understand you do have some guns. Right?"

"We found guns in the cabin but those belong to the traffickers."

"Have you identified the weapon that was used to kill the couple?"

"Bruce should be able to tell us that, hopefully sometime today. His forensic pathologist should have a report shortly. What we found in the cabin were two handguns with machine gun conversions, nine assault weapons—AR-15s—and two Uzis. What I learned last night from a police officer who happened to overhear two men talking about their efforts to sell guns to the people connected to the cabin is that they have been directed to deliver goods on Fridays only."

"Have those guys been picked up?"

"No. I wanted to wait for you and your team because the two men the deputy overheard may lead us to whoever is running the operation. We have the license plates and other information on the two men overheard so we can follow up with them if you wish."

"Not yet," said Pete, "you're right—they may lead us in the right direction. Good thinking."

"After my next meeting, which will be short, I'll drive you out there, Pete, and show you the route the traffickers have been using, which is a seldom used back road. Then I'll show you our own way in, which is a recently developed utility road into the Forest that the traffickers are unaware of—at least so far. It's an old deer trail that we have just had cleared for this reason and this only. No one else is allowed access."

"So my people will be able to set up surveillance without being seen? Are you sure?"

"To the best of my knowledge? Yes. But this will be a first, so we have to be very, very careful."

"That's an understatement, Sheriff. The AR-15 is a mass shooting nightmare and the top-selling weapon in the country." Pete shook his head. "Do you have any leads? Bruce seems to think you do."

"Yes but no confirmation yet. We learned yesterday that there are two men, a father and a son, longtime summer residents out of Chicago and heirs to one of the logging fortunes up here. In fact, it was their great grandfather who gifted the Robideaux Forest to Loon Lake years ago.

Pete's face showed a reaction that Lew couldn't quite interpret. "You wouldn't be talking about the Olssons by any chance?" he asked.

"Yes," said Lew in surprise. "Grant Olsson and his son, Andy. No proof they're the ones, but we've learned they're dealing in guns. You know the Olssons?

"Yeah. Years ago I ran into old man Olsson and a man he introduced as his son. This is a good thirty-plus years ago and that old guy can't be alive. Grant was his son's name. That guy would be in his late seventies, maybe eighties today."

"That's him. Grant is Andy's father."

"I was still with the Rhinelander Police Department at the time. This was before I joined the FBI. And we had had complaints from the Olssons' neighbors out there on the lake where they had that big mansion of theirs. The neighbors complained that they could hear gunfire all the time. Turns out the old guy actually had his own private shooting range for machine guns."

"Machine guns? What? How? They were illegal, weren't they? Am I missing something?" asked Lew.

"No. Very illegal, without question. But money had crossed hands and those of us in the police department at that time were told to mind our own business. So that was that. I've checked and I can assure you there is no private shooting range today. That disappeared when the old man died. But I understand that Grant Olsson inherited quite a collection of antique guns and that he—"

Before Lew could speak, Pete said, "—And he *sells* antique guns."

Lew was quiet. After thinking over Pete's news, she said, "Well, at least they don't make Uzis anymore. AR-15s are scary enough."

"Now who the hell told you they don't make Uzis these days?" asked Pete with a look in his eye and a tone that told her she was dead wrong.

Lew shook her head. "How can they get away with this?"

"Good question," he said with a grimace. "What we know currently is that there is a new gun, the Uzi PRO, which is a modern version of the original Uzi. The new version was released in 2021. The Uzi PRO has updated features that make it easy to use and it's available in nine millimeter with different barrel lengths. We're seeing it show up among Mexican cartel users. Not a good sign."

It was clear to Lew that Pete really knew this stuff. She opened her mouth to say something but Pete held up his hand.

"This gets tricky," he said. "There's more. While it's illegal to manufacture, sell, or possess these Uzis in the United States, it *is* legal to sell manuals, tooling, and templates to complete conversions. So fact is, Sheriff, we could see Uzis being trafficked by your guys. That's why I'm here and three of my agents are flying up from Chicago over the next couple hours. But . . ." With a slight smile on his face, Pete paused.

"But what?" asked Lew.

"But that doesn't mean we can't put two hours in on the Prairie tonight if we get started early. Who knows? We just might meet Bruce and his new bamboo rod." And with that Pete winked.

CHAPTER

17

THE MOMENT PETE Cooke left Lew's office after agreeing to meet up late that afternoon, she hurried to alert her deputies and the Loon Lake Police Department about the upcoming surveillance and potential arrests under the direction of the FBI. Even though Pete and his fellow FBI agents were now in charge due to the nature of the assault weapons involved, Lew needed to be sure that all law enforcement personnel were alerted to the proceedings and ready to step in if the situation became confrontational. She wanted no one hurt or caught off guard.

It was nearly four o'clock when she called Osborne to let him know the plan and ask him to meet up with her at the Prairie. "You haven't met Pete Cooke yet, Doc," she said with a chuckle, "so I think we're in for a treat. He and Bruce have known each other—and fly fished together—since they were in their teens. I'm expecting to see two grown men regress to the age of fourteen as they battle over what size Royal Wulff to tie on."

"Sounds entertaining," said Osborne, "Heading to the Prairie right now?"

"Be there in half an hour. Got to run out to my place to get Nellie," said Lew, referring to the beat-up, fifteen-year-old four-wheel drive pickup she used for fishing. "Then, since he lives right down the road, I'm going to stop by Rob Mason's place, see if Ben is doing okay and ready for the tournament this week. That young Ben was bullied by that jerk running a sports betting operation still bugs me. If he approaches any of those boys again, I plan to file a formal complaint. Shut him down."

* * *

Rob Mason, a pen behind his ear, answered the door of his modest three-bedroom house that overlooked Tamarack Lake, which was less than a third of a mile from Lew's farm. "Good afternoon. Rob, got a minute?" asked Lew, noting the surprise on his face. "I won't stay long, just checking in on young Ben."

"Hey, Sheriff, come on in," said Rob. Looking over her shoulder, a smile spread across his face as he caught sight of her truck. "Haven't seen your Nellie in a while. Someone going fishing?" He waved for her to follow him into his kitchen where he had been busy with paperwork that was strewn across the kitchen table.

"Yep," said Lew, answering his question in a sheepish tone, "can't help it sometimes."

"Hey, I understand."

"Ray told me about Ben's run-in with Andy Olsson so I wanted to check and see if either of you two have heard more from the guy? When is that tournament?"

"It starts this Friday. But no, I think he got the message," said Rob. "If not from Ben, Ray sent a clear message via Andy's brother, Eric, I'm sure. No, Ben seems good. I'm not worried, and I know Ray is working with the boys tomorrow, too. Mind if I ask where you're fishing tonight? These early fall evenings are good for hatches, don't you think?"

As he was talking, Ben walked into the kitchen. He appeared so surprised to see Lew in her fishing garb that she leapt to answer the question in his eyes before he could ask it: "Fly fishing the Prairie with some old friends tonight," she said, smiling. "I came by to wish you good luck this weekend."

"Oh," said Ben with a shy shrug. "Y'know, Dad tried showing me how to use a fly rod last summer. I kinda had a hard time with it—the casting. But I'd like to try it again someday."

The eagerness in his voice prompted Lew to say, "Really? You want to try sometime? I'll give you a casting lesson one of these days. That's what I do when I'm not working, y'know."

"Oh, gee, that'd be cool. Dad's good but—"

"Tell you what," said Lew. "I'm meeting up with a good friend who's trying to decide between buying himself a new bamboo rod or a graphite one so there's going to be some good talk about fly rods and casting.

Do you want to come and watch? This guy's no expert so it'll be a good learning session."

Lew glanced over at Rob, "What do you say? Want to follow me out and listen to me argue with Bruce Peters?"

"Bruce Peters?" Rob was impressed. "I know that guy. I'm happy to listen to anything he's got to say. The man is an expert—"

"Not on fly rods," said Lew with a laugh.

CHAPTER

18

Lew pulled into the clearing at the Prairie River with Rob and Ben Mason right behind her. Though her invitation to follow her and listen as she advised Bruce on casting fly rods had been impromptu—and surprised both father and son—all it took was one glance at his son's eager eyes for Rob to say, "We're in, Sheriff. I can't think of anything I'd like better than for Ben to watch you show Bruce Peters how to fly fish." He grinned. "Who knows? Might change his life."

Osborne had already arrived and was pulling on his waders. Just past his Subaru was parked an unfamiliar SUV. As she was climbing out of her pickup, Lew heard rustling sounds, then someone shouted, "Hey, Sheriff. . . ." The voice came from behind the open door on the driver's side of the SUV and as the door slammed shut, a head popped up. Lew wasn't surprised to see Pete Cooke.

"Where's your best friend?" she asked Pete.

"He's on his way. Should be here any minute. We wrapped our meeting less than an hour ago and I know he wanted to check and see if that autopsy report was in."

"Was it?" asked Lew sitting down on a nearby log to pull on her waders.

"Haven't heard yet." Pete reached into his car for a rod case and his fishing vest.

Even as Pete was speaking, Bruce Peters's car pulled in. The driver had barely turned off the ignition before he leaped from the car and ran down the path to the streambank. He stood for a long moment, looking to his right and his left as he studied the surface then turned to dash back up to where everyone had been standing in silence watching him.

"And the good Lord says. . . . ?" Lew asked him.

"Mayflies and midges by the millions," said Bruce, his brows bouncing with happiness, "Dry flies, for sure. I'm going with my Royal Wulff. Y'know, I forget how nice it is to fly fish in the early fall like this. The water is down, the breeze light. Should be easy wading."

Noticing Rob and Ben for the first time, Bruce stopped short, saying "Hey, who are you folks? You look familiar, old man." He stuck his hand out to shake Rob's. "Have we met? " Before Rob could answer, Bruce had stepped sideways to stand in front of Ben, saying, "Now you look *real* familiar. Weren't you just written up in the Wausau newspapers? You're one of those kids in that high school muskie tournament, aren't you? Why the heck are you here?" Bruce glanced over his shoulder at the Prairie as he said, "No muskies in this joint, dontcha know." With a wide grin and a bounce of his eyebrows, Bruce stuck his hand out to shake Ben's.

Ben took Bruce's hand, a shy look on his face as he said, "That's me but my dad, here, he's a fly fisherman and a friend of the sheriff's. She said it was okay that we could come and watch for a little while. Dad tried to teach me to fly fish but I had a hard time casting with the fly rod compared to how easy I can cast for muskies—but I only tried once."

"Hey, Ben, I know what you're saying," said Osborne from where he was leaning against the back of Lew's pickup. "For years, I fished muskies exclusively but I always wanted to try fly fishing. And you are so right—it is quite different from your muskie spin fishing. That might be easier but, believe me, knowing how to cast a fly rod is well worth it. Not that difficult once you get the hang of it."

* * *

As he was talking, Osborne remembered that not trying fly fishing wasn't exactly his choice: his late wife, Mary Lee, had made it clear that "if you spend one more dime on stupid fishing junk, I'm divorcing you." He could laugh about that memory today but she had been very serious. She had hated his fishing—the money he spent (even though it was the only thing besides a deer rifle that he spent money on and, as a dentist, he had made plenty for her to spend on the household and whatever else she wanted or needed) and she had hated the time he spent fishing—time away from her (the very time that kept him healthy, by the way). But now life had changed. Now Lewellyn Ferris was the woman in his life and Lew? Well, she made fishing—and life—a delight.

* * *

"But I know exactly what you mean, Ben. Casting for muskies *is* easier because spin fishing uses a heavy lure with a fishing line that is basically weightless. When you cast for a walleye or a musky, it is the weight of the lure that propels the line. Fly fishing, on the other hand, uses a *heavy* line with a relatively *weightless* trout fly. So the emphasis is on the casting, which moves the fly to the fish. *Not the lure—the cast.*" Realizing he'd gone on too long, Osborne decided to shut up.

"Before anyone says another word," said Lew, "I have a non-fishing question for Bruce. Any news from the McKenzie autopsy? Sorry," she said, glancing at the others, "but I need to know."

"Yes, the killer used a Glock."

"I'm betting we'll see plenty of those tomorrow," said Pete.

"A Glock, huh. Thank you. That's all I need to know," said Lew, "tonight is for fishing, tomorrow for guns. And let's get started, guys, because I have to quit early. Most of us need a good rest tonight."

"I have a fishing question," said Bruce as he unscrewed the cap of one of the two rod holders that he had pulled out of his trunk. "I think I've learned enough from my fine teacher here, Sheriff Ferris," he said, bowing in Lew's direction, "that I would like to upgrade from my beginner's fly rod to a new one. Question is: Do I go bamboo or graphite?"

A moment of silence followed his question.

Pete was the first to speak up. "Are we talking 'classic' bamboo'? Because you're crazy if you are, Brucie," he said, calling Bruce by his nickname from childhood. "The damn things take months to make, cost way over a thousand dollars and remember how upset your old man was when you broke the tip off his prized rod trying to get a fly unsnagged in the stream that day?"

"Thanks for the memory, Bud," said Bruce, faking a pout. He looked around at everyone watching him. "Yeah, years ago when Pete and I were still learning to fly fish, I snuck my dad's bamboo fly rod out of the garage and ended up damaging the darn thing. Pete's right: Dad was pretty upset. He had to send it to some famous rod maker in Montana to get it fixed . . . he did not leave it to me in his will." Bruce paused, looking so sad Lew wasn't sure if he was pretending or genuinely upset at the memory.

"Oh, come on, no need to make a big deal over this," said Lew as she unscrewed her own rod holder. She glanced over at Ben who was paying close attention to the conversation.

"You may find bamboo works for you, Bruce, but take your time and try plenty of rods before you make a purchase, and I'll tell you why.

"It isn't about bamboo or graphite so much as what rod works for you. What rod feels like an extension of your own arm."

As she was talking, she was putting her fly rod together and had walked down to the streambank, still talking as she reached for a trout fly that was resting on the small pad affixed to the left pocket on her fly fishing vest and got ready to tie it on. Everyone followed her movements, glued to every word and watching while she threaded the fly line through the guides on her rod.

"Over the years I have fished with both bamboo and graphite rods," said Lew as she raised her right arm for a roll cast. "I choose graphite and I'll show you why: the light weight and fast of recovery of graphite makes casting easy for me. And that's what I look for in a fly rod: ease. What I like is how exceptionally quick my rod sends the fly line to the target. And what more could you want?"

"I could want your skill," said Osborne, muttering to himself.

After throwing him a quick smile, Lew walked into the stream and started to cast. Then she paused and turned to look back at Bruce. "Okay. Here's your assignment: Go to your favorite fly fishing shop—maybe the one in your home town—and ask to try a selection of their bamboo and graphite rods outdoors. Once you try a number of each, you'll find one that feels right. That feels like it's part of your arm. Keep trying until you feel that. Trust me, when that happens—and it does happen—you'll know you've got the right one."

Ben, who had been listening and watching Lew, turned to his dad and said in a low tone, "She's so smooth how she moves. . . ."

"Like dancing," said Rob, nodding as he agreed.

"Yeah, good way to put it," said his son, not taking his eyes off Lew.

After a few beats, Ben raised his voice to say, "Sheriff Ferris, I have a question. . . ."

"All questions welcome," said Lew, turning away from him as she shot her fly line upstream.

"Is fly fishing fun? I mean, I know how fun it is to hook a big muskie. But is it the same with those little teeny trout?"

"Tell you something, young man," said Lew, trying hard not to chuckle. "Trout may be 'teeny' but they're tough. And smart. Something you're gonna learn in life is don't judge a fish or an animal or a human by how they look. Trout may be small but they will give you the same fight a muskie will. . . ." She cast again before saying, "Since you brought it up, I'll tell you the most fun I've ever had in the trout stream had nothing to do catching a trout. . . ."

She paused before continuing and as she cast again before answering Ben, her audience of four, anxious to hear over the burbling Prairie River, moved closer to the streambank.

"About ten years ago," she said as she was reeling in. "I was fishing the Kinnickinnic River with one of my Trout Unlimited friends on a Saturday morning in the late spring. The day was sunny, just a light breeze, and as I'm walking upstream, I happened to turn around and," Lew paused in her casting and turned to face Ben, "I'll tell you I could not believe what I saw. There had to be a million mayflies in the air and trout jumping to catch 'em! I am not exaggerating. I must have seen a *hundred* brook trout leaping into the air. My friend and I—we were so astonished. We just stood with our mouths open and watched. An amazing sight.

"So, Ben, you asked about fun. Fly fishing for me is less about the catching than the feeling of forgetting. Forgetting how long I've been standing in place, how long I've been casting. It's about losing my sense of time, my meetings, my list of what to do next. It's about being in a beautiful place. And that's what I call 'fun.'"

Pete was the first to applaud. The others followed.

Minutes later as Pete, Bruce, and Osborne followed Lew upstream, Rob and Ben walked to their car. Draping his arm across his son's shoulders, Rob asked, "Think you'll give it another try one of these days?"

"Jeez, what do you think, Dad?"

CHAPTER

19

IT WAS TEN minutes after five Friday morning when McBride County Sheriff's Deputy Jack Curran woke up to find himself needing to use the outhouse as soon as possible. He looked over at his colleague, sitting in a nearby chair, but Deputy Rice had nodded off too. Taking care not to wake the other man, Deputy Curran hurried outside the old logging cabin to the outhouse.

When he was done, he strolled back across the clearing to the small cabin and let himself back inside, still without waking Deputy Rice. What he did not do, as he crossed the clearing, was look up to the northeast. If he had, he would have seen the taillights of a black van crossing the meadow behind a stand of young balsam.

Minutes earlier—as they would find out later—as the driver of the van was heading toward the old cabin via a rarely used logging lane, he had been surprised to see a light moving near the outhouse. The light was from Deputy Curran's headlamp, which he wore to keep from stumbling in the dark. The driver paused his van and waited, watching. He had used that outhouse and knew there was no built-in interior light.

When he saw the man emerge from the outhouse, he turned around and left the area as fast as he could. Once he was on the county road, he reached for his cell phone.

CHAPTER

20

TO HER SURPRISE, Lew was not the first to arrive in her office at five forty-five the next morning. It was clear Pete and the other three FBI agents had been strategizing for at least an hour.

"We're planning to monitor all traffic heading toward that cabin, starting about twenty miles out in every direction," said Pete, showing her a hand-drawn sketch. "Be easier to manage inspecting vehicles and people one on one rather than conducting surveillance at the cabin only."

"Safer, too," said Lew. "Who knows what kind of weapons you're going to find."

"Yes," said Pete, in agreement. "We'll be working with your deputies, too, Sheriff, but we're taking the lead today.

"Fine with me," said Lew. "I've already informed everyone of that. Keeps my people out of harm's way."

"I'll be at the cabin," said Pete. "I'm relieving your two deputies shortly and I'll take over. I know to park my car a good half mile down that utility road so it'll be out of sight."

"As are the deputies' squad cars," said Lew. "When you see the squad cars this morning, you'll know you're a half mile away. I've made sure no vehicles can be seen from the cabin."

The excitement was palpable as the men left her office. Both Lew and the FBI agents knew this could put a significant dent in gun trafficking across the upper Midwest.

As he walked out behind the others, Pete said to Lew, "If you keep your cell phone nearby, I'll send you an alert when we have our first encounter. I'll keep you updated as the day goes on, too."

"My deputies and I are standing by if and when you need backup," said Lew. "Like I said earlier, I want no one to get hurt."

"This isn't our first rodeo, Sheriff," said Pete with a reassuring pat on her shoulder. "Should go pretty smooth."

* * *

Two hours later, Lew had not heard a whisper much less seen a blink on her cell phone. She kept checking to be sure the local fiber optics network hadn't suddenly gone awry. But nothing. By nine, she was anxious. She couldn't imagine that some of the couriers weren't on their way. Shouldn't one or more of the agents watching the roads have seen something?

Pete called her at ten. "Nothing. Not even a teenager breaking the speed limit on their way to school. You must have had bad intel."

"I can't believe it," said Lew. "That police officer knew what he heard and the clearing in front of the old cabin showed plenty of tire marks in recent weeks. Someone has been coming and going and it isn't the forest rangers."

"I believe you. Someone got wind of our plan—they tipped 'em off. Or else they were watching and saw one of our agents."

"Boy, I find that hard to believe," said Lew.

"We're not giving up," said Pete, "we'll be keeping an eye on traffic and this cabin until dark. Who knows? Maybe they plan to make their deliveries after dark. . . ."

* * *

At seven that night, Pete gave up. Lew was downhearted. "I feel like I put out a false alarm, Pete," she said, apologizing.

"No, you didn't," he said. "Something happened. Someone overheard one of us talking, someone got a signal. Remember, these guys are trafficking in very dangerous guns. They know they are targets. The slightest whisper will alert them. No, you and your deputies did nothing wrong. Those guns have to go somewhere. Let's wait and see where they try to deliver next."

"Damn it—something has to break."

* * *

Dismayed, embarrassed and frustrated, Lew arrived at Osborne's in bad humor. "Take it easy, Lewellyn," he said, "you had a bad day. You did nothing wrong."

"I'm not sure about that," said Lew, "not sure at all."

"Well, you need something to raise your spirits and it is Friday night, so I have a suggestion. . . ."

His suggestion didn't solve the problem but it helped a little: He treated her to the Friday fish fry at the Loon Lake Pub. It helped, too, that bluegills were on the menu.

CHAPTER 21

LEW GAVE UP hoping for positive news from Pete. Either she had a bad source through the Loon Lake Police Department or the gun traffickers had somehow been alerted. Either way, nothing had happened and Lew couldn't help feeling guilty that Pete and his FBI colleagues had spent so many hours traveling, waiting, planning. She sure didn't think she deserved a nice dinner.

At the sight of the tension in Lew's eyes and features, Osborne said in a teasing tone, "Any chance you can let go of work for an hour and enjoy these perfectly sauteed bluegills?" He kept his voice kind but badgering. They were sitting in a booth in the Loon Lake Pub, which was crowded and noisy, as it always was on Friday nights.

Lew gave him a sad smile as she said, "I know, Doc. You're right. I need to let go of my frustration but we were just so sure—"

Osborne patted her hand, saying, "Eat."

Just as she raised her knife and fork, she heard a woman's voice say in surprise, "Officer Ferris? Is that you? Holy cow? Wow, how long has it been?"

Lew's head shot up. All it took was a second for her to react at the sight of the friend she hadn't seen in years. Lew immediately slid out of the booth and scrambled to her feet.

"Connie Steadman, doggone, it's been a while. How have you been?" Turning to Osborne, Lew said, "Excuse me, Doc. Connie is an old friend. Years ago we trained together." She turned back to the tall, dark-haired woman who was standing beside their booth, a wide smile on her face. "Golly, Connie, we haven't seen each other in—what—fifteen years? Not since that last seminar we attended at the state crime lab down in Madison. How the hell are you?"

"Oh, hey, I don't want to interrupt your meal," said Connie as she gave Lew a quick hug. "But I'm great and you look pretty darn good yourself."

"Where are you working?" asked Lew, "somewhere down state?"

"No. I went private three years ago. I had been a narcotics detective in Milwaukee, did a lot of undercover, but as soon as my kids were off to college, I decided to make some real money for a change."

"Ah," said Lew, "private investigator?"

"No, I'm an E.P. Agent." Lew gave her a confused look. "An executive protection specialist—a glorified security guard for well-heeled clients. Well-heeled is putting it mildly." Connie dropped her voice as she said, "I work for a guy worth millions.

"Go," Connie pushed Lew back into her booth, "back to your dinner. Where can I reach you one of these days? Still with the Loon Lake Police, I assume?"

"Nope, I'm sheriff," said Lew, "you can reach me at the McBride County Sheriff's Department. And where can I reach you? Who is this rich guy you're working for?"

Connie's face froze and she backed away. Lew realized she had asked the wrong question.

"Never mind," said Lew, trying to sound cheery. "You call me."

"Deal," said Connie, giving her a quick handshake as she disappeared into the fish-fry crowd.

"I guess I asked the wrong question," said Lew, a little chagrined, as she raised her fork over her plate.

"Well, I'm sure privacy is critical to a position like that," said Osborne as he used a piece of sourdough bread to clean every hint of bluegill from his plate.

"Privacy or secrecy?"

"Hey, the real question, Sheriff Ferris," said Osborne, "is apple pie or chocolate cake for dessert? No sharing tonight. I want my whole piece of pie." And he gave her a happy grin.

Half an hour, later as Lew was tackling the last crumbs of what the Loon Lake Pub called their Chocolate Delight, Connie Steadman came rushing past their booth. This time as she passed by Lew, she leaned down, her eyes serious, and whispered, "They know it's you."

Before Lew could say a word, she was gone.

"What?" Lew gave Osborne a stunned look. "What was *that* about?"

Osborne was silent for a long moment. Then he said, "You know exactly what that was, Lewellyn. A warning. By the way, you're staying at my place tonight."

* * *

Hours later, after Osborne had drifted off to sleep, Lew crept out of the bedroom and over to the desk at the far corner of the living room where she had set up her laptop. She knew she couldn't sleep until she had learned more about Connie Steadman and her recent assignments.

What she did know was they were still good, even close, friends though they didn't see each other often. It was during the first seminar they had attended years ago that the two of them discovered they were both going through difficult divorces from men they had married when they were just twenty years old.

* * *

Connie had been in couples therapy with her husband when she learned he was still being unfaithful. Lew's husband was faithful but only because he continued drinking so heavily that he was incapable of straying. Lew, who had just joined law enforcement and was still in training, was also grieving the loss of her teenage son, Chris, who had been killed in a bar fight. Connie, meanwhile, was in the midst of losing her mother to cancer.

It was after sharing what was happening in their lives that the two women had looked at each other and started laughing. "We have to laugh, Connie," Lew had said as they burst out. "I mean, life is so grim right now the fact is—it can't get worse. Right?"

"You are so right. Well, I guess we could turn into criminals, but what good would that do?"

"True . . . I think. . . ." Lew had paused before saying, "Look, you and me, we're strong, sensible women and we will find our way through this, right?"

"That's why we're here," said Connie. "That's why dark as the day may be—you and I—we know we'll get through this. . . ."

"And have fun. Right?" Lew had laughed again even as she felt tears in her eyes.

"I'm glad I met you, Officer Ferris," said Connie, wiping away her own tears, "now let's survive and go have a good time. Onward."

And with that they had sealed their friendship.

* * *

It was nearing midnight when Lew gave up. She had been able to track Connie's career from her days working narcotics to a seven-year stretch on human trafficking in the southern states. That is when Connie's trail disappeared. There was a hint of her working with someone down in South America but no details. All she found after that was a profile on LinkedIn of Connie as president of her new business, Steadman Executive Protection and Global Event Security. No mention of where she is working at the moment or even how to reach her. The only contact information appeared to belong to whoever was running the company office. That contact couldn't be reached until Monday morning.

Fatigued at last and ready to go back to bed, Lew was walking across Osborne's living room when she stopped to look for the moon through the huge picture window overlooking the lake. She heard the glass shatter before she saw the shards flying at her.

CHAPTER

22

"DON'T MOVE, LEWELLYN," said Osborne from where he was standing in the bedroom doorway. "Stay very still. You're lying in a pool of shattered glass."

Having closed her eyes to mentally check to see if she felt pain anywhere, which she did not, at least not at the moment, Lew did as she was told. She heard Osborne walk away, then return. "I'm throwing down a blanket to cover these shards of glass. Stay still until I tell you to move."

"Don't worry," said Lew as she heard something drop close to her head, "I hear you."

More sounds of movement. "Okay, now roll to your right, then stop."

Lew did as she was told, shifting slowly until she was sure she was all the way onto the blanket. "Don't move yet," said Osborne. She felt his hands dust up and down the outsides of her pajamas. "All right, I'm going to take your hand and pull you up to your feet but be very careful to keep your feet on the blanket."

Once she was upright enough to get a good look around her, Lew gave a sharp inhale. "Guess I'm lucky, huh?"

"Lewellyn, come here," said Osborne, opening his arms and reaching to hold her close. "We're both lucky. *Damn* lucky."

For one of the few times since she had lost her son so many years before, Lew wept.

A loud knocking at the back of the house startled them both, followed by the sound of bare feet rushing through the kitchen toward them, shouting, "Doc, Lew—are you okay? Anyone hurt?"

"Stop, Ray," Lew hollered, "we're fine but there's glass everywhere. Stay where you are."

"But no one is hurt?" Ray was standing at the far end of the living room.

"We're fine but don't come any further," said Osborne. "Lew and I need to get to the kitchen, so hold on while I throw down the rug from the bedroom so it's safe to move around in here."

* * *

Minutes later, standing in the kitchen, Lew rushed through two calls: First, to Dispatch with instructions for the sheriff department deputies on night duty as well as a call to the Loon Lake Police Dispatch unit with instructions to alert all the police officers on night duty; and, finally, she woke up Pete Cooke.

"Take your time, Pete," she said after delivering the news. "Ray Pradt is already outside cordoning off the property next door, which is where the shooter had to be. Ray's dogs would have alerted him if the individual had been anywhere near his place.

"One of my deputies is on the way here and he'll close the town road until morning. Of course, the shooter may have been in a boat or kayak but that's difficult to see at this time of night. By the time you get a helicopter up, they'll be gone. My deputies are checking the boat landings so that may help.

"Ray thinks it's likely the shooter walked along the shoreline on the east side of Doc's place. If they had crossed near Ray's trailer, his dogs would have gone crazy. I'm thinking whoever was out there must have been waiting a while. I don't stay up late that often but tonight I was in the living room with lights on . . . oh . . ."

Lew took a long pause, then said, "You know, now that I think of it they may have followed me and Doc as we drove back here after dinner at the Loon Lake Pub where something odd happened."

Lew told Pete about running into her old friend, Connie Steadman, and how Connie had made the strange remark as she was leaving. "She said, 'They know it's you' and that's all, Pete. Then she was gone. I have no idea what she was talking about but it sounded kind of like a warning. But maybe I'm reading too much into it now that this happened. Think I'm being paranoid?"

"We'll find out," said Pete, "meanwhile, I'm heading your way."

* * *

"Hard for me to tell if a rifle or handgun was used," said Pete after examining the shattered window from the outside and inside. "We'll know for sure when we find the bullets," he said, scanning the wall, across from the window. On the wall was a mounted fifty-inch trophy muskie, Osborne's pride and joy from his muskie fishing days. Pete pulled over one of the wooden chairs from the kitchen, climbed up on the seat and reached for the muskie.

"Sorry, Doc," he said after he had lifted the huge fish down from the wall, "but given that the wall here behind the mount is unmarked and I see a hole under one of the gills, I have to take this guy in to the crime lab. I'll have one of Bruce's people be very careful but I can see that one of the bullets may be hiding behind this hole here." He pointed to a spot just below one of the gills.

"Go right ahead," said Osborne. "The fish will survive."

After stowing the large mount in his SUV, Pete returned to the kitchen where he sat down beside Lew at the kitchen table. He gave her a long look. "You sure you feel okay? You have to be shaken up—"

"For five minutes," said Lew, sounding defiant. "Now I just want to find the creep. I mean, this is only going to make it easier for us to find those gun traffickers. Don't you think, Pete?"

"Oh yeah, and I'm sure they're out there angry as hell. My colleague, Curt, who was watching the county highway this morning said that he had logged two suspicious cars heading this way—likely guys from the cities with goods to trade. That was just after six a.m. and he had pulled out to follow them when both cars very abruptly pulled over, stopped, turned around and headed back the way they came—fast. Something happened early this morning to alert those guys.

"Whoever these gun traffickers are, the fact that their perfect setup at the old logging cabin has been outed has to be driving them nuts. Think about it," said Pete, waving his hands. "They had the perfect cover in a remote place. But now? They can never use that location again. Which reminds me, Sheriff, you know what some of my colleagues call an angry criminal?" Pete didn't wait for an answer, "Stupid. Just plain stupid. Because that is when they make their first—and last—big mistake. As for me? I call 'em 'job security.'" He chuckled at his own joke.

"I'm still wondering what alerted them," said Lew.

"I think I know," said Pete. "I sat down with the two deputies you had watching the cabin during the night Thursday. One admitted he had thought it was safe to use the outhouse a little after five a.m. Friday morning, but my hunch is he may have been out there a little later than that. Given that we've learned there were cars heading that way as early as six, I'm sure someone with the traffickers was likely approaching the cabin to open it up as early and saw someone in that outhouse. That had to scare the bejesus out of them—hence the alert.

"Now, back to what you told me that woman said as she was leaving the restaurant last night, I'll be calling my office in Madison first thing in the morning and have them do a search on Connie Steadman. With her history in law enforcement, chances are good we'll find her. We can check with people who've worked with her. They may know where she is and who her client is."

* * *

It was two a.m. before Lew was ready to head out to her farm. Thanks to the deputies from the sheriff's department, the officers from the Loon Lake Police Department and Pete's people, every inch around Osborne's property and the empty summer cottage next door was lit up like the Fourth of July.

At first Ray was able to take advantage of the mobile lighting units in the summer cottage's parking area. The absent owners had an expansive three-car garage and a newly black-topped driveway, which hampered Ray's work initially. The blacktop was too smooth, holding little evidence of exactly what vehicles had parked there recently. Frustrated, he decided to tramp around the cottage in hopes of other signs of a recent visitor.

That decision turned out to be so fortuitous, he surprised himself. First, near the house and right next to a basement window, he found footprints left by someone wearing boots and moving in such a way that he could tell they had stopped and paused to relieve themselves. He marked the spot as he knew that with no rain in the forecast someone on Bruce's team would be able to get enough material for a potential DNA match. It also meant he wasn't dealing with the brightest bear in the woods. What kind of idiot leaves evidence of taking a leak so close to where they plan to commit a crime?

His grim pleasure was short-lived as he felt overwhelmed by how close his dear friend Lewellyn Ferris had come to death. The moment he realized the shooter's intent, Ray also understood how much he cared for this smart, wise, hardworking woman. Lew might give him trouble for the goofiness of his jokes, but underneath her needling was sincere affection. He knew that she understood, too, how talented he was on the water and in the forest. Those times when he caught her looking at him with admiration after a success in one of their investigations—due to his eyes and ears—made up for all the criticism he had taken over the years from his parents and siblings who never did understand why he chose to live the life he did.

No, Lew's continuing support of who he was and how he thought had saved his life. The most critical moment may have been when he was sitting in his first AA meeting after a rehab stint of his own at the Hazelden/Betty Ford Drug and Alcohol Treatment Center and was asked by another AA member if, given his recent binges after falling off the wagon for the third time, he knew anyone close to him, whether family or people with whom he fished and worked, might continue to feel confident that he could do what he kept promising to do: beat the bottle.

The moment he was asked that he knew one person standing by with hope in her eyes and that was his boss and close friend, Loon Lake Police Officer Lewellyn Ferris. He knew she could see beyond the failures.

That memory of her unstinting support haunted Ray as he moved past the summer cottage and toward the finished stone stairway leading down to the docks, currently pulled up out of the water for the winter, in hopes of seeing more footprints left by the intruder just an hour earlier.

CHAPTER

23

As Ray moved in the dark, now depending on the beam of light from his fishing headlamp, he mentally rehearsed the guidance he'd gotten years earlier from one of the Ojibwa elders the summer he hung out with him and his friend.

"Use your eyes like you're a fox," the old man had said. "A squirrel wants acorns so those are under branches—and you want the squirrel so look under the branches, see the twigs and check to see if they've moved. Are branches or twigs broken? Has the grass been pressed into the earth? Look up to see if a bear has been by? Has a deer rubbed its face and antlers on a tree, leaving a scrape to mark his territory?

"And sounds. Learn the sound of a frightened loon whose nest is being violated by an eagle, the scream of a rabbit losing its head to a great horned owl. The owls have signals that you must learn if you choose to move through the dark. You do not want to surprise a mother bear with a cub: do that and you will die."

Ray had listened to everything the old man said and forgot nothing.

Moving down the stone stairs, he spotted scuff marks of dirt. He fingered one spot: dried mulch. The intruder must have made his way across the lawn, now overgrown, and across the edge of the mulched border, which the careful owner had built to border both sides of the stone stairway. For once, Ray was happy to see a gardener overdoing it when they should have been relaxing and watching the sunset.

The scuff marks continued down the stairs; from there he found footprints running down to the shoreline. Ray turned to look back up the stone stairs. Ahh, he let the beam of his headlight sweep up the stairs he had just come down, and he could see where the intruder had, moments later, given up using the stairs in his rush to leave. Now the footprints ran up the grassy hill toward the parking area.

Ray turned back to the shoreline. He had a hunch what he might find next: if the intruder was familiar with the lake, he would know that it was sandy and shallow for a long way out, so much so that many summer people deplored how shallow it was since they wanted to moor large yacht-like fishing boats or pull their teenagers in wake boats, which need deep water. Loon Lake offered none of those amenities, as it had no drop-off and was only fourteen feet deep at its deepest.

The shooter must have known that, as they appeared to have walked straight into the shallow water along the beachfront, breaking branches off the young arborvitae along the shoreline. Never had Ray been so happy to see a broken branch. The guy had to push through the shallow water no further than twenty feet before he could step up onto Osborne's beach area.

There the beach was sandy and open. Ray saw the footprints as neat and deep as if they had been pressed into a sheet of pastry dough. Standing near to but not close enough to damage the prints, he took a close-up photo with his cell phone, then looked up. Yes! Anyone standing there would have had a clean shot up at Osborne's big window behind which lights still blazed. A .22 pistol or a 30.96 rifle? Either of those would have shattered the window. And how many guys did he know who had one or both of those in his vehicle at all times?

Pleased with his findings, Ray bounded back up the stone stairs taking care not to disturb the scuffs. Once he was back into the parking area, he saw three of the Wausau Crime Lab's investigators just arriving in one van. "Hey, guys," he said and laid out what he had found.

After they looked them over, before Ray could say "see you in the morning," they were off to get more photos.

* * *

Ray hurried the fifty feet down the road to Osborne's driveway, let himself in the back door and found Pete Cooke pouring himself another cup of coffee in the kitchen.

"Any luck?" asked Pete, settling back in a kitchen chair and sounding as if he didn't expect much.

"Yep," said Ray, his casual tone deliberately downplaying how pleased he was with what he'd found. "Got evidence of a vehicle parked next door," Ray nodded in the direction of the neighbor's summer cottage as he was speaking, "and plenty of tracks left by the whoever he is as he ran down to the lake, waded about twenty feet or so and stepped up on Doc's beach where he had a full view of the living room since we know Sheriff Ferris had all the lights on."

He smiled wryly. "Now you know why back in the mobster days up here—y'know, the nineteen thirties and forties—those razzbonyas always built their cottages *off water.* They didn't want to be seen."

"Good point," said Pete. "It sounds like I better head down there and be sure those tracks are cordoned off?" He made a move to stand up.

"Not to worry. Three guys from the crime lab met me by the garage in front of that cottage. They're taking care of it."

"Good work, Ray."

As they were talking, Lew had walked in and heard Ray's remark about the mobsters taking care to build their places off water.

"Ray's right about the window and how easy it was for the shooter to see me. I call it 'Mary Lee's revenge.'"

"Why do you say that?" asked Pete, taken aback.

"Oh, just a silly comment," said Lew, shrugging. "Doc's late wife is the one who insisted on installing that wide plate glass window, which he didn't want. It was very expensive. Doc loves the porch that they built off to the right front of the house, and he had wanted to extend that instead. But he gave in. What he refused to give up was his fishing, which she hated—that and the big muskie he insisted on mounting there in the living room." She shook her head. "But enough about her. I need some sleep. Just waiting for Doc to grab his overnight bag so we can head out to my place."

"More coffee, Ray?" asked Pete, getting up to refill the coffee maker.

* * *

As Lew waited for Doc, she wondered if she would be able to sleep. One thing she knew for sure: Either she—or Pete Cooke—had to find Connie Steadman, and fast.

A few minutes later, as Pete walked with Lew and Osborne to their cars, Lew said, "Pete, I can't thank you enough for getting out here so fast."

"Yes, you can," said Pete with a grin. "When we get this figured out, you, me, and Bruce will head out to the Prairie again. Watching you cast yesterday, I realized I need coaching on my double haul."

Then, leaning down before Lew closed her car door, he said in a low voice, "Be careful, Sheriff. Once they hear they missed you, they'll try again. But you know that." He shut the car door gently.

CHAPTER

24

EARLY THAT SATURDAY morning, the she-wolf was delighted to see her pups tumbling over one another as they raced across the meadow behind the old cabin. For weeks she had scolded them to stay close to her den but now, with very little human activity happening in and around the old place, she didn't worry. No people meant no one trying to shoot her or her youngsters. She relaxed and, feeling good, watched her pups as they played.

* * *

A few miles away, Ray Pradt pulled into the large parking lot at Chippewa Lake. Ben Mason and his teammates were waiting, fishing rods ready. The tournament would start in an hour. Behind Ray, as he walked toward the boys, cars were pulling into the few remaining open spaces and people were walking toward the bleachers, binoculars in hand, ready to observe the tournament action. Even though he was short on sleep, he felt charged and ready to urge the boys on to victory. He tried hard to push his worry over the assault on Lew Ferris to the back of his mind. He was successful. For the moment.

* * *

Back in Loon Lake, Lew was at her desk and feeling remarkably good, given how little sleep she had had. Hoping Pete had managed to get a break—and maybe an hour or two of sleep himself—she decided to wait to check in with him for an update on the ongoing investigation around Osborne's home and the cottage next door. So far, the only news she'd gotten was that two bullets had been found. Both were lodged in Osborne's trophy muskie mounted on the wall across from the shattered window. Lew felt bad about that and hoped that retrieving them hadn't caused too much damage to her best friend's precious memento. Fifty-inch muskies are prized among outdoors enthusiasts, as they are rarely seen, much less caught, any longer.

* * *

The high school muskie tournament was a big draw for visitors to the Northwoods that Sunday morning. For most visitors, that is, except Riley McKenzie. She was focused on something and someone quite different: her mother-in-law's missing AirPods and the person who had killed her.

"Once I found your mom's iPad, I knew we could do this," she had said to Brian, twisting his arm to go along with her plan. She reminded him that when his parents had recently updated their wills, his mother had given Riley a copy of her list of all their passwords saying, "Honey, you and Brian should keep this in your safe deposit box along with copies of our wills—just in case. Not to be morbid but accidents do happen. . . ."

Recalling that conversation, Riley had snorted, thinking "Accidents? Accidents?! Little did her late mother-in-law ever expect to be the target of some crazed killer. That doesn't happen to doctors' wives."

Brian had balked at first, saying, "Shouldn't you just turn all that information over to the law enforcement people? Like Sheriff Ferris? Or the Loon Lake Police? Should we really be doing this?"

"Oh, settle down," Riley had said, "I'm not saying we'll try a citizen's arrest or some dumb thing. We certainly can't do that. Heavens, we're just going to search and see if we can locate Miriam's missing AirPods. When we do, *if* we do, then we call Sheriff Ferris and she will do the arresting. Right now, I can assure you she would think we're asking too much. I mean, very few people realize you can find AirPods this way."

"Oh," Brian had hesitated. "How does it work that we can?"

"Easy," said Riley, holding up his mother's iPad so he could see what she was doing. "Once I enter her password, I have access to her iPhone and her AirPods—see, like this." She hit a few keys, then said, "Now, look where it says 'Directions.' This is identical to how you can search for your missing iPhone."

"I see but there's nothing there," said Brian. "No 'Directions' show up."

"That's why we're going to drive around," said Riley. "We drive up, down and around Loon Lake and the nearby towns until that word—'Directions'—lights up. At least I hope it lights up. That's all we're trying to do, Brian. If we find that, then I call Sheriff Ferris and give her this iPad. That will make it easy for her to find whoever stole the AirPods.

"Brian," Riley said, staring at her husband, "whoever stole the AirPods is who killed your parents. I'm only asking you to drive fifty miles in each direction. Okay?"

* * *

They had been on the road for three hours that Saturday morning. Every fifteen minutes, Riley would refresh the screen on the iPad and press the "Directions" button but nothing had happened. Traffic was picking up as they drove further north, closing in on the small town just outside Chippewa Lake.

Brian pulled into a gas station and while he was filling the tank, he asked the woman at the next pump why there was so much traffic. "Oh," she said, "today's the final hours of the high school muskie fishing tournament. One of the teams will win a hundred thousand dollars, so there is a lot of excitement—big money for high school kids." She laughed. "Eighteen teams from all over the Midwest are competing. As you can imagine, this is a big deal here." And she smiled as she finished filling her tank. "I have a son who wants to compete next year."

As Brian and Riley drove slowly along the outskirts of the large parking area where people had pulled in to watch the tournament finale, another driver was on his way into the parking lot.

* * *

Andy Olsson had decided to join the crowd and observe the final results of the tournament. He had over thirty-five hundred "clients" placing bets on his new sports gambling website—bets specific to this high school tournament, even though he had been advised that he was pushing the law when it came to taking bets on high school events, not to mention in Wisconsin where it was illegal. "Eh, so what," he had said to a friend advising him against it, "let 'em come after me. A gamble is a gamble, y'know. Who the hell cares if it's a high school fishing tournament or a pro football game?"

What he didn't know as he drove along was that Miriam McKenzie's AirPods had fallen out of her jacket pocket when he had moved her body to the other location back in the Robideaux Forest. Her AirPods were under the passenger seat of his pickup.

* * *

It was nearly eleven that morning when "Directions" lit up on the iPad Riley was holding. "Omigod," she said in a burst as Brian drove down an outside lane in the neighboring lot where visitors to Chippewa Lake and that morning's fishing tournament had parked RVs and campers. "Oh gosh, we're getting closer. . . ."

"Call Sheriff Ferris now," said Brian in a demanding tone. "Now, Riley, I mean it. This could be dangerous."

"I know, I know," said Riley, breathless as she watched them get closer to where the AirPods appeared to be. In her excitement, she hit a button on the iPad screen by mistake—a button that caused the AirPods, wherever they were, to make a pinging noise. It was a sound designed to help people locate their missing devices.

Andy Olsson, just pulling into a parking spot a few hundred yards away, heard the strange sound. He turned off the ignition, listened, and leaned over toward the passenger seat. He reached down. No luck. He got out of his truck, walked around to the passenger side. He opened the door, leaned down again and reached further under the seat. His fingers locked on something: a set of AirPods. Looking at them, he assumed they must belong to a woman he had picked up at a bar the previous weekend. Grabbing the AirPods, he locked the truck, walked over to the edge of the parking area and gave the AirPods a high toss over the tall bushes separating the parking lot from the county road.

Riley, meanwhile, was calling Sheriff Lew Ferris.

* * *

Lew, on the way out to Osborne's home to see what, if anything, had surfaced to give the investigators more leads on who the shooter might be, reached for her buzzing cell phone. It was Marlaine from Dispatch: "You gotta take this one, Sheriff." She put Riley through.

"Sheriff Ferris, I think we got him."

Lew recognized the breathless voice. "Slow down, Riley," she said. "Start over and take it easy." She listened as Riley insisted that she and her husband had located the person who had murdered Brian's parents. "We know where he is and we're on our way."

"No, you are not," said Lew. "You will wait for me before you go any further. You said you are near the public landing at Chippewa Lake, right?" She didn't wait for an answer. "One block up into the town there is a BP gas station. I will meet you there in twenty minutes." She clicked off before Riley could protest. Lew spun her cruiser around, turned on her siren, then called Marlaine at Dispatch and asked her to alert two of her deputies to meet her at the BP station.

CHAPTER

25

Connie Steadman, sitting at the kitchen table in the home of Grant Olsson, watched in silence as the old man, leaning forward on his walker, made his way down the path to the massive storage building he had had built in back of the log mansion where he had lived since he was a child. Both buildings hugged the shoreline of the large lake, which had made it easy for Grant's pilots to land his private seaplane, which had been kept in a hanger inside the storage building back when it was first built. The seaplane was now long gone, sold when Grant lost his millions in the dot-com debacle of the early 2000s.

The building, which was now nearly empty aside from a tractor used by the groundskeeper, an old ATV and various pieces of lawn equipment, had recently been outfitted with shelving and storage units for a new business belonging to Grant's son, Andy. Another room, smaller in size, belonged to Grant's own business.

That business was built on Grant's longtime obsession with antique guns. When Connie was hired by Grant's late wife, the idea was to keep the aging millionaire, who was nearly ninety, safe from people looking to exploit the old man. Grant had inherited nearly five hundred million dollars from his father and grandfather and, never having had to work, wasn't the best at handling his investments. In fact, during the dot-com crisis he had invested with an old boarding school friend only to lose almost everything. It was the recent and unexpected sale of the family's interest in the Rhinelander Paper Mill that had restored a small part of the family fortune, but only enough to pay for Grant's care and to support his modest venture selling antique guns.

Evelyn, his late wife and four years younger than her husband, had been the family business manager. When she learned she had terminal cancer, she hired Connie Steadman to be Grant's E.P. Agent. But while she didn't expect Connie to provide more than security around the home or when Grant wished to be driven somewhere, she had told Connie that if she suspected he was "being taken advantage of," she should alert their son, Eric. Since then, Evelyn had died shortly after the dot-com debacle—an event that Connie suspected had hastened her death. She had told Connie she felt it was her fault: "I thought he and his old friend,

Fred, were buying antique guns—not stocks! Why didn't I ask more questions?.

Connie, as a bystander, had assumed that after their mother's death both sons were aware of their father's finances, especially as Evelyn had made a point of her confidence in her oldest son. "Eric has my brains," Evelyn had said without even a wink. She had also told Connie that while she was close to her oldest son, she failed to understand why Andy had turned out to be such a rude, unkind person.

As she got to know the family, Connie could see that Andy was closer in temperament to his father, who was not an outgoing person and seemed to have little use for his oldest son. She wondered if he had been warmer in his youth or if it was the family money that had attracted Evelyn. *Whatever*, she once said to herself, realizing that the Olssons would need a heavy dose of family therapy if they were ever to figure out why they were who they were.

When she met Eric, a tall, engaging man who loved the outdoors and would include ten-mile runs every time he visited, she found him to be an easy, likable person. When he first took over managing the family finances after his mother's death—an instruction Evelyn had left in her will, Connie could see that he did indeed have his mother's business acumen: the old woman was right.

Also Eric, unlike his father and brother who had never attended college, had gone to Harvard and then to Harvard Business School. After graduating from the business school, he had insisted on making his own way in the world of commercial banking, from which he had recently retired. Then he was hit with his own family tragedy when his wife died of an aggressive form of breast cancer. His two grown daughters, also athletic like their father, were now in grad school and single. Though they lived near their dad down near Chicago, they also enjoyed catching up with their dad up north. All three loved running, biking, and the outdoors.

Connie enjoyed the young women. Like their dad, they were bright, friendly, and outdoors enthusiasts. Meanwhile, Eric had begun to visit more often. Even though his home base was in Evanston, he had been doing his best to have a warmer relationship with his father. With Andy? Not so much. That didn't seem possible.

The more Connie came to know Eric, the more she liked what she saw. He was, as an adult, quite unlike his father and brother in that he had no interest in hunting and guns. A kind man, she had found him to have an easy sense of humor and a sensible approach to health issues, including the dementia that his father was showing signs of.

Eric was a man around whom she had grown to feel comfortable sharing any concerns she had, which he appreciated hearing.

Andy, on the other hand, was always rushing somewhere, spoke to her in curt tones and struck Connie as almost preying on his father.

"That one son demands money from his old man all the time," she had recently confided to a close friend. In fact, the demands had become so constant that she was about to share her opinion with Eric. All that had kept her from doing so until lately was how well she was paid, and a fear of losing her job. With her own son, her youngest, having one year left in college, she had resisted taking an action that might cause her to lose her job—and private security work paid significantly more than law enforcement.

Now, however, her concern had reached a point that she felt it mandatory to say something. At first, when Andy started showing up with assault rifles to sell by piggybacking on his father's antique gun website, she had believed him when he said that he was following the law and that his market was people who felt strongly about gun rights. But it had alarmed her when he had angrily denounced "that crazy liberal Sheriff Ferris who runs that committee," saying that wanted all gun ownership regulated by the government. "That woman is trying to shut my business down," he insisted.

Connie knew gun ownership was a political issue across the country and she saw his interest in the assault rifles as a natural result of his father's fascination with the antique Uzis, which were approved for ownership but not for use. But when he had mentioned the name of her old friend, Lew Ferris, she had felt the urge to let Lew know she didn't have a friend in Andy Olsson, which is why when she had unexpectedly run into Lew, she was happy to be able to alert her.

But her concern had mounted as over the last two days as she had watched Andy arriving with his pickup loaded with more gun cases than usual. The one time she had slipped into the storage building to see what he was delivering she had been shocked to find crates of new Uzis as well as what appeared to be ghost guns. This was too much for Connie, who, after all, had been a law enforcement officer.

Now that Eric was due to arrive from Chicago for a short visit with his father and to "rescue Mom's family albums," she had resolved it was time to risk her job and say something.

CHAPTER

26

EVELYN RYAN OLSSON had never planned to raise a murderer. She hadn't even planned to become a member of the Olsson family, a family famous in the Northwoods of her youth as being "outrageously rich."

It had started her fifteenth summer. A slim teenager with a soft, quiet beauty of which she was totally unaware, she had been sitting on a beach towel at the Loon Lake public beach with two girlfriends when she heard a boy's voice calling, "Evie, hey, Evie Ryan—come here and see my new kayak. Wanna ride?"

She didn't ask how he knew her name until after they had gotten married three years later.

Only then did she bring it up saying, "You know, Grant, I've always wondered how you knew my name that day. How did you?"

"That day—hell, girl. I'd known your name for a year, since the first time I saw you at the Memorial Day parade in Rhinelander that year. I had kind of noticed you a year or two before when our family was up for the summer and you would be at the beach or in the grocery store with your mom. You were just so pretty. I always asked people what your name was."

"Oh," said Evelyn, taken aback, "but nobody calls me 'Evie' except you."

"I don't call you 'Evie,'" Grant had said with a grin, "I call you 'Evie Sweetie' like when I say, 'Hey, Evie Sweetie, want to snuggle up?'"

Now it was Evelyn's turn to grin and give her new husband a kiss on his cheek.

* * *

Their early years were good years. But even with the arrival of their two sons and the challenge of decorating the large older brick home in Evanston, Illinois, that Grant had bought for them, Evelyn was bored. She had always wanted to go to college, but Grant had pressed her to marry him right after high school. She didn't realize until later that that may have been his way to avoid the draft during the Vietnam War.

At first, as their sons headed off to preschool and kindergarten, she started her own interior design business. She was soon up to her ears with five homes to be decorated from porch to kitchen and living/dining areas to bedrooms. She had talent, that was obvious. But when those houses were completed and even as she was besieged with requests from other homeowners, she wasn't happy. The fact was that she loved numbers and logistics. She began to badger Grant to let her go to college.

"Sweetheart," she had said, "I can go part time, I have very nice babysitters, and you won't even know I'm spending time in the classroom. C'mon, ple-e-a-s-e. I want an accounting degree. Just think. Once I have that I can help you make money with the family trust."

The odd thing was that Grant himself rarely worked. He had money in the bank from the family trust and he had a title as Vice President of the family's "company," which was really just the name of the trust—the Robideaux LLC. Grant was a tennis player and someone who enjoyed time with his longtime buddies, guys from the private boarding schools he'd attended. Bridge and poker held his attention when he wasn't batting balls on the tennis court.

Finally, he agreed to Evelyn's request and the family adjusted as she spent half days in school at Loyola University in Chicago. She loved it, and she learned that her hunch had been right: she was a natural with numbers.

As the years went by, she became Grant's chief advisor, taking over from the investment firm that had been managing the trust; at least that was her impression until the year 2000 when Grant insisted on managing the investments for a time. She had been happy to step aside "for a short time" as she had not been feeling great and needed "a little more rest than usual."

Something else bothered her, too. The behavior of her sons, Eric and Andrew—well, not Eric so much.

* * *

From his early days, even in the stroller, Eric had seemed to be much like his mother: quick to smile, an easy learner and a child who spoke in sentences before the age of two. He was a happy kid who loved to curl up beside his mom as she read to him. In elementary school, he had easily mastered his numbers and writing cursive. More important, he got along with the other kids and often stepped up to help the one or two who might be having problems.

"Your Eric is such a sweet boy," more than one mother had told her. "Just the other day, my Jeffrey was being bullied by that big Jackson kid and your son stepped in to stop it. He took the risk of Billy Jackson beating *him* up instead. I mean, my son and his father want to do something special for Eric."

Evelyn was so proud of Eric. Andrew? Not so much.

The frustrations started early. Was it colic? Evelyn couldn't tell, nor could the pediatrician. But Andrew seemed to hate sleep. The only time he did settle down during his first year of life was when he was allowed to fall asleep on his father's chest. In preschool, he was the child who took everyone else's Legos or Play-Doh or beach toys. He was such a burden on the preschool teachers that Evelyn resorted to hiring a child psychiatrist to try to improve the child's approach to other children. Did it help? No. In fact, he was asked to leave. Years later he would brag "I'm the only kid who ever got kicked out of preschool." That was followed by a proud smile.

When Andrew hit second grade, he insisted on being called "Andy," which was fine with Evelyn and Grant. But when he snuck into his classmates' desks to steal crayons and colored markers, he was called "Andrew" again. He was not an easy kid and Evelyn could not fathom why.

One of the worst things he did was in sixth grade, and it was a harbinger of his high school career. A girl in his class was caring for a baby robin that had fallen out of its nest and broken a wing. She would bring it to class on a pillow and, periodically, take a short break to give it some food or water from a dropper. The little bird was thriving. Soon she could wear it on her shoulder as the bird's tiny claws were comfortable on her shirt, so she would sit in class with the little feathered guy right there with her. One afternoon she was standing in the lunch line, the baby robin snuggled under her shirt collar, when Andy walked up and punched the bird against her shoulder so hard that the bird fell to the ground, dead. The girl was hysterical and crying. The teacher, who had observed Andy's move, told Evelyn that he stood back grinning. "Your son thought what he did was acceptable," the teacher told her. "He needs help."

* * *

Things got worse in boarding school. Even as Eric sailed through, earning straight A's and playing basketball and soccer, Andy lasted about a month or two in each of the three schools he attended before being kicked out. In one, he was caught stealing a laptop computer from one student; in another, he was discovered cheating on several exams; and in another, during his junior year, he was buying beer and weed off campus to sell to his roommates. But the episode that froze Evelyn's heart was when she learned he was accused of sexually assaulting the younger sister of one of his roommates.

Bottom line: Andrew Olsson earned his GED at home via correspondence classes, with the help of a paid tutor.

* * *

Through all his youngest son's episodes of bad behavior, one person was only mildly critical: Grant.

"I don't understand you," Evelyn had said to her husband, demanding he punish Andy in some way. More than once, in fact numerous times, she had called Grant out saying, "Grant, you have got to do something or Andy will think he can always get away with being mean (or stealing or cheating or whatever depending on Andy's most recent escapades) to other children. . . ."

But Grant and Andy puzzled everyone by getting along surprisingly well. And it had everything to do with guns. It started when Grant shared his interest in antiques guns with Andy when the boy was six or seven, and it escalated when the two began hunting together.

Deer, bear, and turkey were their targets of choice but, unlike traditional hunters who take care and pride in dressing their kill, Grant would always hire someone else to do the difficult work of skinning, gutting, and dressing their prey. Why? What was it about hunting that made those two happy? The killing.

* * *

About three years into their marriage, Evelyn had realized that her attractive, mild-mannered, adoring husband was not very bright. She could see how his lackadaisical approach to the management of the family trust by an outside firm might put the money at risk but she also saw something else lacking in Grant: empathy for other people. When it came to their relationship, she realized he loved her not because she was a bright, smart person but because she was pretty. Pretty and, maybe, a good cook. The realization made her wonder if divorce might not be a good option, especially after she got her accounting degree.

But there were benefits to her marriage that she appreciated. Having grown up in a family that struggled to make it on her father's income working in construction, the fact that she and Grant had no financial problems was a significant relief. Also, as she got to know the other families around them, especially the parents of children in school with hers, she could see that most marriages seemed to be lacking perfection. So she told herself, "You know, Evelyn, no marriage is perfect—so buckle down and shut up."

And that is what she did.

* * *

So it was that when Evelyn learned she had terminal breast cancer, she waited a month, hoping the diagnosis had been wrong, before making a call to her son Eric. When she admitted to herself that her disease was terminal, she asked him to make a special trip up to the family summer residence, which had now become home year-round for Grant and herself. The day Eric arrived, she told him what the doctors had said: that she had maybe two weeks, maybe two months left. She then gave him the codes allowing him access to the family trust saying, "You will find approximately twelve million dollars, which should more than cover your father's care and leave you with a nice inheritance. Andy has been such a trial for me over the years that I know this sounds cruel of me but I'm leaving him a modest amount—nothing like what you will get."

Eric, after assuring his mother that he would see that his father received excellent care, sat down to open his laptop computer and review the contents of the family trust. During his years in investment banking, he had often discussed the stock market with his mother, conversations that left him confident she knew what she was doing.

But that afternoon, he found nothing.

"Mother," he called out to Evelyn who was resting in her bedroom, which was right down the hall. "Can you give me the access codes again? I seem to have made a mistake."

He tried again confident his first try had held an error. But no. The trust site came up empty.

* * *

Evelyn was stunned. She managed to make her way down to the storage building where Grant was busy cleaning an antique deer rifle. She asked if he was aware of any changes to family trust. At first Grant tried to tell her it was none of her business but when Eric broke into the conversation, he admitted what he had done.

"Your mother was in the hospital having tests," he said to Eric, "when my good buddy, Fred Danner, said he knew how we could make a killing. So I pulled everything out to buy what Fred was buying. . . ."

"I see," said Eric, "are you aware the market crashed two days ago, Dad?"

"Maybe," Grant kept cleaning his gun.

Eric was quiet for a long minute, then he said, "I'll arrange for you and Mom to move down to Evanston and live with me. Sound okay?"

But in a stroke of luck, two days before the moving van was set to arrive to pack up the Olsson belongings in their lovely log mansion on the lake, Evelyn got a call that the family's interest in the Rhinelander Paper Mill, which had recently been sold, was being wired to their bank account. The Olsson share of the paper mill, which had been in the family for nearly one hundred years, was worth 1.6 million dollars. Evelyn and Grant did not have to move.

All that Evelyn could say on hearing the news was: "This family has too much good luck." Eric agreed. No one mentioned the entire debacle to Andy.

CHAPTER

27

Pulling into the BP station, Lew spotted Riley standing outside the car at the same moment that Riley saw her. Waving as she ran toward Lew's cruiser, Riley said, "Sheriff, we found the AirPods." She pointed down the street toward the entrance to the Chippewa Lake boat landing. "If you'll follow us," she said, sounding breathless as she spoke fast, gesturing with an iPad in one hand, "I got directions to it right here." She waved the iPad.

As she was talking, two of Lew's deputies pulled into the gas station and stopped next to her cruiser. "I'll be right behind you in a minute, Riley," said Lew, "hold on while I give my deputies an update." After instructing the deputies to follow her, the four cars left the station and headed to the parking area for RVs and campers. When Riley's car came to a stop and Riley jumped out, Lew was right behind her. The two women stared at Riley's iPad screen, which indicated they had to be standing very near the AirPods.

"I don't see anything," said Lew. Then she looked toward the bushes and trees along the side of the lot. Riley punched a button on the screen and suddenly they heard a pinging noise. Brian, who had climbed out of the driver's seat, started walking in the direction of the pinging. He stopped, bent over and was about to reach down when Lew shouted, "Stop! Please don't touch anything. Stand back, Brian, please." Lew pushed ahead into the bushes to stop beside Brian. The AirPods lay at his feet. "Don't touch a thing," said Lew, heading back to her cruiser for a paper evidence container.

After slipping on a pair of nitrile gloves, she picked up the AirPods and slipped them carefully into the evidence container. "Fingerprints," she said to Riley and Brian who had been watching in silence. "It's a long shot, but Bruce and the Wausau boys are checking every crack and seam in the McKenzies' SUV. If their killer left a trace, the crime lab will find it—and these could be a match."

She turned to her deputies and said, "Let's photograph all the license plates parked here right now. Who knows? When we do find who killed the McKenzies, we may also find that the same individual happened to be here watching the tournament."

"It's my fault we can't find that awful person today," said Riley, sounding close to tears. "I must have hit the sound button by mistake when I was following 'Directions' on Miriam's iPad. If I hadn't done that. . . ." She started to cry.

"Riley, stop," said Lew, "you did darn good to get us here. Finding these AirPods is critical to our investigation. This confirms that the person who killed your in-laws is still in the area somewhere. They haven't left. So please know that this is a huge help."

Lew walked over to Riley and gave her a hug. She could see through the young woman's tears how bad she felt.

* * *

Down at the large, six-dock Chippewa Lake boat landing, a stage had been set up. The top three catches of the day, which ended the tournament were hanging over a temporary podium. Three groups of young men stood to one side waiting for the ceremony to begin. Two television crews were scrambling as the reporters readied their microphones. Spectators were gathered along the docks and the shoreline. A happy buzz of voices, along with the sound of outboard motors on the fishing boats gathering offshore to watch, filled the air. A sunny, cloudless sky blessed the late morning.

Lew spotted Ray standing off to the right with the cluster of high school kids he'd been coaching. She recognized Ben Mason. The boys looked excited. Had they won?

Before heading over to join Ray and his muskie fishing team, she called Pete Cooke to see if he had any updates on the search for who had shot at her the night before.

"No, sorry," said Pete. "I will call you the minute we know more." After sharing with him the news that they had found the missing AirPods, she decided to take a few minutes and watch the ceremony.

* * *

The tournament winners were announced to cheers and clapping. Ray's team came in second, winning fifty thousand dollars. "Not bad. Congratulations," said Lew, walking up to Ray and the boys after the announcements had ended. "Splitting fifty grand makes for a very nice Saturday," she said, grinning as she shook each boy's hand.

"And they get to keep the fish," said Ray. With that, he brought both palms to his face and let loose with a loud, lingering loon call. Lew had to laugh as he got almost as much applause from the remaining crowd for his loon call as they had given the winning team.

After all the happiness and celebration, Ray pulled Lew aside to say in a quiet voice only she could hear, "Ben has been watching the crowd, Sheriff. He's convinced that Andy Olsson, who tried to scare him into fixing his catch for his sports gambling operation, would show up."

"And has he?" asked Lew on sudden alert.

"Not that we've seen. I've stayed close to Ben just in case," said Ray. "I get a hint that jerk is here, you'll hear ASAP."

"Good. I'm about to head back to my office. We had a false alarm, kind of, that we may have located a set of AirPods that may have been taken by the person who killed the McKenzies."

"Oh, yeah?" Ray asked. "But no sign of them?"

"Oh, we found the AirPods, but they had been tossed into the bushes when whoever had them heard a sound that had been activated by accident. So whoever that person is was here watching the tournament all right. Very disappointing but I'm hoping we get prints off them. Ray, we are so close. . . ."

"So you think they were in this crowd?" asked Ray. "Now who would that be? I would expect a gun trafficker to be long gone from the Northwoods."

"I agree. So what is keeping them here? And why come after me? Pete Cooke and the FBI investigators are the ones to be wary of. If they get whoever is behind all this, he's facing federal charges. They'll put him away for years."

* * *

Sitting in the small apartment behind the kitchen and utility room of the Olsson's log mansion, Connie Steadman felt her impatience growing as she waited to hear signs of Eric's arrival. She knew his flight from Chicago to the Rhinelander airport had been delayed, but that wasn't unusual and rarely meant more than an hour's delay.

After serving the elderly Grant his evening meal and making sure he was comfortable in his bedroom suite, the family housekeeper had left for the day. It was Connie's responsibility to provide security for the old man during the night, but since he had a habit of retiring right after his evening meal, she found her evenings free. Tonight she was determined to let Eric know what his brother was up to.

It was nearly eight o'clock before she saw the lights from Eric's rental car and heard the front door open and close. Connie hurried through the kitchen and front hallway. "Hey," she said when she saw Eric about to go up the wide staircase leading to the upstairs bedroom suites, "we need to talk for a minute—"

"Is Dad okay?" Eric paused, alarm in his eyes.

"Your father is fine. It's another matter that I think you should be aware of."

"Let me check on my dad and, assuming he doesn't need me for anything, I'll be right down, Connie. Sorry to have arrived so late. By the way, have you eaten? I'm starving. Care to join me at the Loon Lake Pub for a late sandwich? We can talk then if that's okay with you?"

"That'll be fine," said Connie, feeling relieved. This would give her plenty of time to describe why she was finding Andy's behavior so alarming.

* * *

Back at her office, Lew shuffled through the reports that had been stacking up on her desk since early in the week. As she was reading the last one, her personal cell phone rang.

"Lewellyn," said a familiar voice, "aren't you hungry? It's my night to cook but the window repair crew is still working. Afraid we need another option."

"Oh, gosh, Doc," said Lew, "I didn't realize it was this late. I'm hungry, too."

"Well, we have an invitation. . . ."

"We do?"

"Ray is treating his team and their folks to prime rib night at the Loon Lake Pub. We're included if you're up for it. I told him I wasn't sure. You didn't get much sleep last night."

"That sounds terrific," said Lew. "Now that you mention it, I think I skipped lunch. Let's do it. And if the window guys are still working later, let's plan to be at my place again tonight."

"Pick you up in ten minutes," said Osborne.

CHAPTER

28

THE PUB WAS bustling. "This place is so busy," said Eric to Connie as he led the way in. "I don't know if I've ever seen it so busy."

"Fishing tournament's top three winning teams and their families are here," said the young hostess in a proud voice as she showed Eric and Connie to one of the few open tables. "Everyone is celebrating tonight."

After placing their drink orders, Eric gave Connie a sympathetic look, saying, "Okay, I'm ready. Are you resigning? If so, this will be just one more of my day's catastrophes. . . ."

"Oh, heaven's, no," said Connie, managing a laugh in spite of her anxiety. "No, no. But I am very concerned about your brother. He's behaving in a way that could lead to serious legal issues like"—Connie hesitated before deciding to be blunt—"even prison."

"Damn it!" Eric threw up his hands. "I tried to tell him that sports gambling was an iffy proposition, especially when it comes to fishing tournaments. Frankly, it's iffy any way you look at it, which he has already learned the hard way—but that's another story. And I gotta tell you, Connie, Andy is not going to listen to me. He never has. He is my father's son and we could not be more different."

"This isn't about gambling. Well, not really," said Connie, keeping her voice down as she leaned over her glass of club soda. "This is about guns—"

"Oh, yeah, my dad's antique gun business? What? Is he helping himself to the profits? Surprise. I know he took over running Dad's website so that leaves everything wide open, y'know."

Eric was talking so fast Connie didn't try to stop him.

"Let me tell you, Connie, Andy has always taken advantage of my old man. Right after Mom died and Dad lost everything in the dot-com debacle—Andy maneuvered Dad into appointing him the executor of the family trust even though I was running it. The only good news is that our trust got some money out of the sale of the Rhinelander Paper Mill, which meant there was some money to cover Dad's care. . . ."

Eric sighed and looked away before saying, "Smartest thing I ever did was step away from this crazy family and head off to college far away. Boy, was that a lucky move."

Before he could say more, Connie said, "Eric, you've got to hear what I have to say about the guns that Andy is handling. Please listen because these are not your father's antiques. He is trafficking in *illegal* guns. Here's what worries me and, keep in mind, my background is in law enforcement. I know this territory. . . ." Relieved to see she had Eric's full attention, Connie paused for a split second before continuing.

"Over the last couple of days your brother has made at least two trips a day delivering guns to your family's storage building. He's got a whole section separate from your dad's antiques where he has been stashing AR-15s and other illegal guns. And I mean amazingly dangerous guns like new Uzis. Those are highly illegal. I saw so many illegal guns when I checked the space out earlier today that I'm beyond worried."

She gave Eric a long, serious look: "I think your brother is *trafficking* guns. He's using your father's antique gun business as a front. And, Eric, I'm sorry but I have to report this. I felt I owed you the courtesy of telling you what I'm planning to do tomorrow."

Eric stared at her, silent. "I am so sorry," said Connie, "but Andy's actions are too dangerous—for all of us. I mean, who the hell is he working with?"

Though Eric had appeared stunned at first, his expression soon changed to resignation. Then he nodded and said, "You're right. This can't be allowed. First thing in the morning, I'll take a quick look at what you're describing, then together we'll contact whomever you suggest. The cops? The sheriff? You know law enforcement, I don't."

"The McBride County Sheriff's Department. They'll know what to do. Also, the sheriff is someone I know personally," said Connie, "we trained together years ago. She'll be fair."

Head down, staring at his drink, Eric said in a quiet voice, "This is good. And in a strange way this is the first reassuring thing I've heard all day." At Connie's look of surprise, he said, "Let me tell you why I flew up here. It has nothing to do with guns, but the guns don't help."

Before he could say more, their food was delivered. After poking half-heartedly at the sauteed walleye on his plate, Eric raised his eyes to hers. "Andy placed some bets over the last two weeks that wiped out what was left of my father's estate. The family trust is gone again! For the second time! Dad lost it first in the dot-com debacle, then we lucked out with money from the sale of a long-time family interest in the Rhinelander Paper Mill. Not much but enough to cover Dad's care. And now that's gone. Pfft! Gone—just like that."

Connie stared at him. "Your brother could do that on his own?"

"Dad made it possible. Something else, too. I don't know how closely you've observed my father's behavior recently, but he's slipping. When I talk to him on the phone, I'm hearing more and more signs of dementia. Would you agree?"

"Definitely," said Connie. "That's why I feel my job as his security professional has been critical. As your mother said, 'he needs protection from people who might take advantage.'"

"Like my brother. You know, Andy has never made an honest buck. Oh, he had a couple jobs out of high school like working at a gas station or construction, but he always got fired. Then he got into gambling, which is why he's so big on the sports betting. But, of course, he keeps losing money. I wouldn't doubt that Andy has *stolen* more money than he's ever made."

It was Connie's turn to stay silent.

Then Eric said, "I'm here to tell Dad we have to sell the property. That will help me pay for his long-term care. Though it's now heavily mortgaged thanks to Andy, I'll be able to help out financially. What I can't—and won't—do is give Andy a dime. He can take care of himself, dammit." As Connie watched, Eric attacked the walleye on his plate as if the poor fish was the source of the problem.

"He may be sitting in prison," said Connie, keeping her voice low and hoping to calm Eric down. She sympathized with his anger, which was spilling out as he talked.

"When was the last time you saw Andy?" she asked.

Eric shook his head as he said, "Last week. I ran into a guy I know, Ray Pradt, at the sporting goods store in Loon Lake. He's a fishing guide who took my dad, me, and Andy out for a day hunting muskies years ago. He told me Andy had been trying to intimidate one of the boys in the high school fishing tournament. Pushing the kid to fake his catch so Andy could fix the bets on the tournament. I ran into Andy right after that and I told my brother to lay off the kid or I'd turn him in. Not sure if I would really do that but it sounded good." Eric gave a sad smile.

"Well, this is a lot to take in," said Connie, setting down her fork. "How soon do you plan to sell the property?

"I hope to put it on the market sometime in the next couple weeks. I happen to know that one of my dad's old friends has moved into a senior living center over in Minocqua. Dad might like to live there, too."

"And his antique gun business?"

"Time to give that up. At least I hope he'll agree."

A sudden squeeze of her left shoulder caught Connie off guard until she heard a familiar voice exclaim, "Connie Steadman—I have been looking for you . . ."

* * *

Minutes later, after introductions, Lew and Dr. Paul Osborne pulled back chairs to join Connie and Eric at their table.

"So, Connie, do you mind if I ask where you're working these days?" asked Lew.

"Of course not. I should have said something the other night. I'm an E.P. agent for Grant Olsson, Eric's father." She nodded toward Eric as she mentioned his father.

"And what exactly is an E.P. agent?" asked Lew. "Sorry, but I'm not familiar with the term."

"Executive protection specialist. Eric's late mother hired me, as she felt he might need support and protection. He's in his late eighties and he is—was—quite wealthy. She felt he might be preyed upon. You know how that can happen to elderly people."

"I do. But what did you mean when you alerted me the other night saying, 'they know it's you.'"

"I meant that Grant's son, Andy, who has been working in his father's business of selling antique guns has been quite vocal about the restrictions you have put on gun sales in the region."

"Me?" Lew said sounding surprised. "These are state and federal regulations."

"My brother is not a reasonable man," said Eric, interrupting. "Connie has just informed me that aside from helping my dad with his business, my brother has been buying and selling illegal guns. Sheriff Ferris, I'm more than willing to share what Connie has told me she has seen and heard in the last couple days."

"This is disturbing news," said Lew. Glancing from Eric to Connie and back to Eric, she said, "Someone tried to kill me last night." As she was speaking, Lew got up from her chair. "What's your brother's full name?"

"Andrew Olsson."

"Will you excuse me for a few minutes, please. I'll be right back." Lew hurried across the room to the hallway leading to the restrooms. Once in the privacy of the Ladies Room, she locked the door, called Dispatch and asked to be put through to Dani Wright.

"Dani, sorry to interrupt your Saturday night," said Lew, on hearing Dani's voice. "I need you to run a check ASAP on a guy and see what license plates are issued to him. Pete Cooke called me late this afternoon to say that the house next door to Doc's had a door camera that registered a black pickup parked in that driveway late last night. We think whoever was parked there is the individual who waded along the shoreline and shot at me through Doc's big window. I need to know if that black pickup belongs to an Andrew Olsson." And she spelled out Olsson.

CHAPTER

29

"DON'T WORRY, SHERIFF," said Dani when Lew called her later that night. "I had just gotten home from a really bad date, so your timing was great. Got my mind off the jerk I had dinner with." As Dani chatted on, Lew checked her watch. It was shortly before ten o'clock and she had called Dani to apologize for pulling her into the investigation and ruining "your lovely Saturday night." A "lovely" Saturday night? Apparently not.

Hoping to end the conversation with Dani soon, Lew glanced over at Osborne who was sleeping soundly beside her. She hoped that keeping her voice down wouldn't wake him. He was still tired from Friday night, too.

After they left the Loon Lake Pub with Eric and Connie, Osborne had dropped Lew back at her office parking lot so she could get her cruiser and drive out to the Olsson property to meet up with Eric and Connie.

* * *

While waiting for Lew to arrive, Eric had hurried up the stairs to check on his father while Connie did a quick check of the downstairs rooms. Once he could see that his father remained sound asleep and that Connie could find no evidence of Andy coming or going in the house since they had left, Eric settled down to wait for Sheriff Ferris to arrive.

Twenty minutes later Lew drove up and the three of them walked down the lighted path to the storage building. That, too, was quiet with no sign of a recent entry. A quick check by Connie of the last four hours recorded on the video door camera showed minimal activity around the main entrance: no humans but three curious does and a young buck. Otherwise no sign of Andy, coming or going. Once that had been confirmed, Connie led Lew and Eric over to the room that Andy had commandeered. To everyone's surprise it was not locked.

As Lew entered, she saw stacks of crates, similar to the ones she had seen in the old logging cabin. The first crate she checked contained an AR-15 and two new Uzis. The next crate she opened held devices designed to make semiautomatic guns fire like machine guns.

"I've seen enough," said Lew to Connie and Eric as she pulled out her personal cell to call Pete Cooke.

"Pete, I know it's late but this is an alert. I've just been shown a collection of guns, which are being bought and sold by an individual named Andrew Olsson. He goes by Andy and he is not here at the moment. I think it wise for you and your agents to take over with surveillance at this point. Sound good?"

"Good?" said Pete. "*That's* an understatement. This is what I've been waiting for—but," said Pete, his tone changing from excited to concerned. "Can I assume you're okay? Not in danger at the moment? Or do you need me to call for back-up ASAP? Tell me where you are and how fast you think we can get there. . . ."

"I'm fine at the moment but keeping a close eye out."

"How far from Loon Lake are you? I can be ready to go in five minutes. My men, too."

"See you in half an hour," said Lew and gave him the location for his GPS.

* * *

Once Pete and his three agents arrived, Lew gave them a quick tour of the room's contents. She had opened two more of the crates, and now she reached in to pull a gun out from each. The expressions of the faces of Pete and his men answered any questions she may have had: they were stunned.

"I want this guy," said Pete. "I want him and I will see that he's put away for years. What we're seeing here puts so many lives—especially people in law enforcement—in danger. Unconscionable."

* * *

On hearing that, Lew was ready to find and arrest Andy at his home immediately. She turned to Eric for directions.

"His place is over on Sunset Lake. That's the next lake over from here, maybe five minute drive," said Eric. "He moved there right after Mom died. The lake is small but Dad bought him a new log home on four acres."

"I know Sunset Lake," said Lew, turning to Pete. "I'll drive. You tell me if I handle the arrest or the FBI."

"The FBI," said Pete. "What I see here tonight violates federal law—"

"And the guns I found at the old logging cabin were on state property," said Lew. "I'm your backup."

* * *

The two of them set off. The driveway from the county road to Andy's home was long and dark. All the windows along the front of the modest log home were dark. After trying the doorbell on the front porch and getting no answer, Lew and Pete walked around the house but found no lights on in the back or along the sides. Not even a motion sensor light came on in the backyard down near the path leading to a dock.

Lew called Eric for more information. "Do you think we might find him in a bar somewhere?"

"No idea," said Eric. "Andy doesn't tell me much. I know he's had some girlfriends off and on. Could be he's spending the night with someone?"

"I want him under surveillance, Pete," said Lew. "You need your men at the storage building. I'm calling Dispatch and ask to be put through to my deputies working tonight. We can handle this end."

In less than ten minutes, Lew had reached two deputies and arranged for them to monitor Andy's driveway and house. "Please keep both myself and Agent Pete Cooke informed of any sign of anyone approaching," she had added.

* * *

As they headed back to the Olsson's storage building, Lew's cell buzzed: Dani Wright. Lew put her on speaker so Pete could hear what she had learned.

"Yes, Sheriff, you nailed it," said Dani. "License plate registered to Andrew Olsson, home address on Sunset Lake in McBride County, town of Piel. It matches the license plate on the pickup shown in the video door camera on the house next door to Dr. Osborne's. He had to turn around in the parking area, so there is a clear visual."

Lew and Pete's eyes met.

* * *

Minutes later Lew pulled her cruiser up to the storage building where Pete's agents were busy cataloguing the collection of guns, "Some of these have come in from

Mexico," said one of the agents. "Not only illegal but a new model of machine gun we haven't seen before. Your guy must have excellent contacts to find these."

It was close to ten o'clock when the fatigue hit. With an apology, Lew told Pete she had to take a break. "Lewellyn," he said, "you've been going on very little sleep the last twenty-four hours. Get out of here—now."

"I'll be at Doc's place," she said, "his house is closer. All I need is a couple hours sleep—"

"Look, I'll call the second this Andy shows up—here or at his house. Now go get some sleep.

"All I need is an hour," said Lew.

"No, you need more than that," said Pete walking her to her cruiser. At the look on her face, he added, "Nope. Do not argue."

* * *

Lew woke to a nudging on her left arm. Opening her eyes, she saw Osborne standing with a tray in his hands. "Good morning, Lewellyn—better sit up before your eggs get cold." He bent over to kiss her forehead.

"Oh no," said Lew, pushing herself up onto her elbows and brushing her hair out of her eyes. "What time is it? I don't have time to eat, Doc."

"Settle down and be quiet," Osborne said in a mock serious tone. "First, it's early—five a.m. Second, you haven't had a call from Pete. So eat first, then run."

Gulping her orange juice and savoring the bacon and eggs, Lew felt restored. When her offer to take the dishes to the kitchen was turned down, she rushed to grab a quick shower and get dressed. Still no call.

Getting into her cruiser to head north, she called Dispatch with assignments for two more deputies. In addition to the surveillance on Andy's home, she wanted the entrance to the Olsson estate watched so that Pete and his agents would be alerted if anyone besides her turned off the road and onto the driveway leading to Grant's mansion.

As she headed that way, she called Pete's number. "We're here, inside," he said. "No sign of Andrew Olsson . . . yet. Sleep well?"

"I did, thank you. I'm heading your way. I think there is parking behind the main house, so unless he shows up and you alert me in the next ten minutes, I'll pull in there."

"See you soon. Enter the house from the back and stay there until we know more. I checked a short time ago and made sure that door is open."

"Got it," said Lew. She waved as she passed one of her deputies who was already parked far enough from the entrance to the Olsson property to be hidden but close enough to see any vehicles arriving. Lew kept going and turned in at the decorative wooden plaque that marked the driveway.

The Ohlsson property looked quiet—no cars parked in front of the main house or the storage building. She drove around the house to park in the far back where she knew her cruiser couldn't be seen from out front. Once inside, she made her way through the utility room and down a long hallway to the kitchen. Eric and Connie were sitting at the kitchen table drinking coffee.

At the sight of Lew, Eric held a finger to his lips. She took a chair beside him and sat down. "My father is still asleep," he whispered. "Not sure what's going to happen but they don't want me to wake him."

"He usually sleeps late like this," said Connie, checking her watch. "It's only six-thirty."

With fresh, hot cups of coffee in front of each, the three of them sat in silence, each lost in their own thoughts. The view from the kitchen was to the east, where the autumn sun was rising. The morning was overcast, but a small tear in the blue-gray clouds off to the right let a stripe of vibrant orange slip through. Meanwhile, to the far left, as if to contradict the Great Planner in the Sky, the clouds were opaque. Soft and dove gray, their billows crowded close as if determined to hide the rising sun: a reminder to onlookers that there are no easy answers in life.

* * *

Connie sipped at her coffee, planning ahead. Late the previous evening as she was about to retire, Eric had stopped her at the doorway to the small apartment she was using at the back of the big house.

"I know my mother appreciated how much you were able to help her out with my dad during her last few months," he had said. "With the way things are going now, I'm sure you realize I won't be needing your services."

"Of course," Connie had said, "but—" Before she could say more, he handed her a check. Connie looked down, expecting to be paid through the end of her contract, which was up at the end of the year. She would be owed five thousand dollars. The check was for fifty thousand.

"Oh, no, there's been a mistake," she said. "I'm only owed five thousand and, really, you don't even owe me that much. I'm happy to finalize my work here very shortly."

"I owe you more than I can say," said Eric. "You deserve what I'm giving you. Without you alerting me to Andy's hijinks, who knows what might have happened. My dad could have been murdered by some of these bad actors Andy is dealing with."

Connie didn't add that she couldn't agree more. The more she had been around Andy lately, the more she had heard him ranting about Lew Ferris and the people in law enforcement regulating guns, she had begun to worry for her own safety. She was, after all, a retired police detective.

"If you're sure," she had said to Eric as she held the check, "I want to thank you. For the record, this will help me pay my son's last college bill." She gave him a happy smile and went off to grab a few hours of sleep.

Before she closed her eyes and nodded off, she planned her next move. Since Eric would no longer need her services and her son's college costs were covered, she was free to do whatever she wanted. She knew she wanted to work but she also knew she wanted to work with people she liked, people she respected. Who came to mind first? Lew Ferris, of course.

She decided to check it out in the morning. Did the McBride County Sheriff's Department have any openings for experienced detectives?

* * *

Eric sat quietly at the kitchen table, thinking over everything that had happened the night before. First was the shocking discovery of all the illegal weapons in the storage building. As if that wasn't enough, Sheriff Ferris had pulled him aside to tell him that Andy was her prime suspect in the murders of Dr. John and Miriam McKenzie.

"I heard from Bruce Peters who runs the Wausau Crime Lab that they have matched your brother's DNA, which was found near the McKenzies' bodies to the DNA in prints on a pair of AirPods that he had must have found in his truck after moving the victims' bodies. Mrs. McKenzie's family knew she always had them on her, using them or carrying in her pocket. I drove out with their daughter-in-law and her husband after their iPad indicated the AirPods were somewhere in the parking lot near Chippewa Lake, where the high school muskie fishing tournament was taking place. Someone parked there had dropped them or tried to throw them away. We found the AirPods, which is how we've been able to match the prints."

"Oh my God," Eric had said, "I've known my brother was a cheat and a thief. I've known he was mean as hell and would never hesitate to take what he wanted. Sheriff, I recently learned he stole every dollar from our family trust and lost it gambling. But killing people?

I had no idea he would go that far. That poor family. You'll have to let me know how I can help. . . ."

Lew had then said in a low, measured voice, "And me. He tried to kill me two nights ago."

Eric stared at her.

"Though I don't think he knew the details, he was aware it was me and one of my deputies who discovered what he was doing at the old logging cabin in the Robideaux Forest. He had restored it and was using it as the delivery site for his gun trafficking. The old place is hidden so deep in the Robideaux Forest that few people knew it still existed.

"It happens to be near several wolf dens, which is how the McKenzies stumbled on it, surprising Andy at a time when he was there and had the place full of weapons."

"So that's why he killed them," said Eric.

Lew nodded.

"And you?" Eric's eyes searched Lew's.

"I was lucky," said Lew, "just damn lucky. I may have moved at the last second when he was firing, but who knows? He got a trophy muskie though," she gave a little laugh, "right under the gills."

* * *

Sitting in silence near Connie and Eric, Lew sipped at her coffee. She felt rested and she felt good. For the first time in a week, she felt close to resolving a difficult chapter in the lives of people she had been trying to help. Riley and Brian McKenzie were two people she had observed struggling to deal with the devastation of losing his parents in such an unexpected, painful way. Riley had been so enterprising in her dedicated search for the missing AirPods that Lew was impressed and wondered what were her career plans? If she needed recommendations of any kind, Lew would like to be first on her list.

Then there was Eric Olsson. What a brave, kind man he is. Even as he is sitting beside her after having heard all the grim news about his brother, he remains calm and ready to help his father again. She had to wonder about the old man. How had he failed his younger son? Thinking back to her struggle to raise her son, Chris, to be a bright, good, honest person in spite of the negative influence of his father, she sympathized with Eric's mother. She had never known the woman but she had a hunch that if they had met, they might have commiserated over the difficulties of raising children. It's one thing to tell someone to "be your best self," but something else to show them how to do that. Even more difficult when someone else can interfere and make bad behaviors seem more fun.

"Ah well, some things can't be changed even though we do our best," thought Lew. "On the other hand, there is one thing I can—and will—change: my life with Doc."

* * *

"Hey, folks," said Eric, interrupting everyone's thoughts, "I just heard something. Dad's up and moving . . . I'll check on him in a minute and get him out of here as fast as I can." He got to his feet.

Right then, Lew's phone buzzed. She saw it was Pete. She signaled for Eric to stay where he was. "Our man has arrived. He's heading to the house," said Pete. "I want him in the building here. If not, we'll stop him if he tries to leave the premises. You lay low, Sheriff."

"Your brother is here," Lew was whispering to Eric as they heard the front door open.

CHAPTER

30

"DAD? READY? BRING a jacket, it's chilly outside."

Silence. Lew, Eric, and Connie sat perfectly still, staring at each other.

"Do you hear me?" the male voice called again from the front hall at the bottom of the stairway leading up to the bedrooms. Louder this time.

"Y-y-e-a-h, be there in a minute," said a faltering, grumpy voice in response.

Without making a sound, Lew got to her feet and slipped quickly into the nearby alcove holding shelves of food supplies and cookware. If Andy were to walk into the kitchen, she didn't want to be seen.

Eric also stood and headed down the hall to the spacious entryway at the front of the house. "Andy, what are you doing here?"

His brother, wearing jeans and a black jacket, stood waiting in the foyer.

"I should ask you the same thing," said his brother. "You didn't tell me you were coming."

Before either one could say more, their father appeared on the upstairs landing, "Eric, what the hell you doing here?" he said in angry voice.

"I arrived late last night, Dad, don't you remember? We're going to see the lawyer tomorrow."

"Oh," the old man hesitated, "that's right. Forgot."

"I always take Dad for breakfast on Sunday morning," said Andy. "C'mon, Dad, you're late." He glanced over at Eric and said, When we get back you can tell me what's up with the lawyer. I'm executor of the trust, you know."

"Oh, sure, that's right," said Eric, sounding hesitant as if unsure what to say or do next. Lew, listening, stayed hidden and motioned to Connie, sitting at the kitchen table with a tense look in her eyes, to stay where she was and remain silent. Lew knew Pete wanted to handle the arrest.

Eric looked up to watch as his father managed to slowly, slowly make his way down the stairs, cane in one hand with the other gripping the banister. He then walked out the front door with Andy, who took his arm. The two men made their way down the front porch's stone steps and along the stone walkway leading to the paved circle in front of the mansion where Andy's pickup was waiting. Andy helped his father into the passenger side, reaching around his waist to give the old man a boost up.

At the sound of the front door closing, Lew had hurried to the front hall and was watching from a window in the living room, which was off to the right.

"Be right back, Dad, I gotta grab something from my office," said Andy, turning away from the pickup to walk down toward the storage building. Eric, still standing in the foyer, started toward the front door as if to follow after them.

Seeing Eric move, Lew said, "No, don't, Eric. Stay right here. Let the FBI handle this."

Ignoring Lew's instructions, Eric continued out the front door and down the path after his brother, saying, "Andy, wait. I forgot to mention something. Hold up for a minute, will you? We need to talk."

At that moment, Pete Cooke appeared in the entrance to the storage building. "FBI," he said to Andy in a loud voice, "Andrew Olsson, you're under arrest."

Andy stopped short. Eric, nearly bumping into him, didn't see Andy pull a handgun out of his jacket pocket.

Lew saw the gun. Without thinking she lunged out the front door toward the two men, her voice raised in a howl as she ran.

Turning around as if to run, Andy reached for Eric who was right behind him. Grabbing Eric around his upper arms with his own left arm and the pistol in his right hand, Andy raised the gun toward Eric's head as he shouted, "Any closer and I'll kill my brother. Got it?"

Pete was backing away when Lew hit Andy from behind at the same instant that Eric yanked his long legs up and twisted to the right, hitting Andy's right arm, which went up and as it bent to one side, his grip on the pistol tightening in a reflex motion to right himself, the gun fired. Eric froze. Andy, eyes wide open, dropped to the ground. The bullet had entered the side of his head.

* * *

Eric stared down at his brother's body. "Did I do that? I didn't do that. Please tell me I did not help kill my brother." He broke into sobs. Pete ran toward him just as Lew got to her feet and Connie ran down from the house.

It was Connie who reached out for Eric, gathering him in her arms, trying to calm him.

Pete knelt down by Andy, checking to see if he could find any sign of life, checking his pulse and for any breath. Getting to his feet, he called for an ambulance. Then he said, "Eric, you did not kill your brother. He had his finger on the trigger when you were trying to struggle free. The trigger was pulled when his arm flailed: he shot himself. It was an accident, and one that was entirely his fault."

As they stood there, the three agents with Pete joined the group. The old man, meanwhile, managed to get himself out of Andy's pickup and walk slowly across the lawn to the cluster of people.

"What's all the commotion?"

Pulling himself together, Eric stepped forward. He looked at his father for a moment, then said, "There's been an accident, Dad. Andy was showing us his new pistol and somehow managed to pull the trigger. I'm so sorry, Dad."

And Eric broke down again.

The old man stood quiet. He looked over Eric's shoulder at the body on the ground. "I keep telling him to be careful with those goddam new guns," he said, shaking his head. "He wouldn't listen. He liked to take the safety off—said he wanted to test 'em. More than once I told him to be more careful . . . now this."

Pete, on his knees, was examining the pistol. "The safety is on the trigger," he said, "All it would take to fire this gun is slight pressure here," Pete held the gun out and showed everyone the trigger's safety lock and how easily it released.

Grant Olsson shook his head, turned and started back up to the house. With nods from Pete and Lew, Eric walked after him.

CHAPTER

31

THAT MONDAY MORNING, the relief in the air was palpable. Bruce and Pete had been busy chatting while everyone gathered around the conference table at one end of Lew's office. At the far end of the table, Dani Wright was leaning forward, eyes fixed on the screen on her laptop.

As Lew took her seat and, glancing out the big windows at the end of the room got a good look at the parking lot, she winced. She couldn't help remembering the sight of the lovely oaks shadowing the lawn that she had enjoyed in her old office at the Loon Lake Police Department. With an inward sigh, she acknowledged that moving up the professional ladder did not guarantee perfection in life or work.

Before she could open the meeting, Ray Pradt walked in. He was wearing one of what he liked to call "my work shirts." This one bore large letters identifying him as JUST ANOTHER FISHERMAN. "Yeah, right," said Bruce, hooting and pointing at the shirt as Ray took the chair beside him.

"Hey," said Ray, happy to be center stage, "did you hear the one about the chameleon who couldn't change color?" After looking around the table to be sure he had the attention of everyone seated there, some holding their breath with a hesitant smile, he said, "he had reptile dysfunction."

"Oh, geez," said Pete with a shake of his head. Bruce let his eyebrows express his mild disgust and Lew said, "Thank you, Ray. Can I start now?"

* * *

A dumb joke, she thought, but a good sign. For the job was done. No more deaths, no more dangerous guns being bought and sold. The old logging cabin was no longer off limits to curious visitors to the Robideaux Forest.

"Dani, you go first," said Lew.

"Thank you, Sheriff," said Dani, turning her laptop so everyone could see the screen. She had anticipated being asked to confirm her discovery, so she had worn her new business suit and had had her hair done early that morning. Being the center of attention was a key driver for Dani; one more reason why she didn't mind Lew needing her to work late on a Saturday night.

She pulled up the video of Andy Olsson's pickup pulling into the driveway of the empty summer cottage next door to Osborne's home, then fast forwarded it to show the pickup turning around, allowing the door camera to catch the license plate. She paused the video and zeroed in on the license plate. "I was able to confirm that the license plate issued to Andrew Olsson was valid and had been renewed three months ago. Any questions?"

"Good work," said Pete. Dani beamed.

"I'm next," said Bruce, brows raised as if to challenge anyone who might get in his way. Then he paused, realizing there was more to be said about the pickup and its driver. In an apologetic tone, he said, "Sorry, Ray, you go first. Why don't you tell us what you found on that property that night?"

"Because I live just two lots away and because I knew the owners of the house had been gone for over a month," said Ray, "I knew when I saw signs of someone having parked in that driveway very recently that we were on to something. I walked down to where the absent owners had pulled their dock up on land for the winter and found obvious sign of someone entering and leaving the water within hours. What I saw next doesn't take an expert: You can't hide footprints in the mud.

"Also the water is only three or four inches deep as you walk along the shoreline toward Osborne's place. Olsson made the mistake of stepping up onto the shore there, too, so more prints. Bruce, back to you, man," said Ray.

"We matched prints from Andrew Olsson's boots to the ones Ray found," he said as he passed three large photos around the table. “This confirms that Andrew Olsson was the individual who shot out the plate glass window in an attempt to hit Sheriff Ferris.”

The room was silent. Bruce shuffled a few papers, then said, “We caught a break when Riley McKenzie, daughter-in-law of the late Dr. and Mrs. McKenzie was able to locate her mother-in-law’s iPad and a list of her passwords. You’ll recall that Riley insisted her mother-in-law would have had her AirPods on her at the time of her death either in her ears or somewhere in her clothing. Aware that AirPods can be located in the same way you can find misplaced iPhones by using other Apple devices, Riley searched for Mrs. McKenzie’s iPad. Once she found it and a list of Mrs. McKenzie’s passwords, Riley and her husband drove around the Northwoods, hoping to pick up some sign of the missing AirPods and, eventually, they did.

“The iPad indicated that someone who had parked near the Chippewa Lake boat landing during the fishing tournament last weekend had the AirPods in their vehicle. Riley, however, made a mistake that turned out to work well for the Wausau Crime Lab. She accidently pressed an icon on her screen that caused the AirPods to make a pinging sound designed to help people find their devices. The person who had the AirPods in their vehicle turned out to be Andrew Olsson. He found the device and not knowing exactly what it was and how it had ended up in his pickup’s back seat, he threw it in the bushes.”

Bruce paused and the room was silent, waiting. "Right," he said, acknowledging what was on everyone's mind.

"We found the AirPods and were able to get prints from those that we could match to prints we were able to locate in two other key places. The first, at the old cabin where illegal guns had been stored. More critical, Andrew had moved the bodies of Dr. and Mrs. McKenzie in the back seat of his pickup. We were able to get his prints off belongings of theirs, which had been thrown into the woods near where the bodies were found. Among several items we were able to find and test was Mrs. McKenzie's small leather purse. No question who had moved that after her death." Again Bruce paused and bounced his eyebrows. "It was Andrew Olsson who moved the victims' bodies. Was he the person who shot them? Likely."

When Bruce had finished, Pete spoke briefly about the alarming number of illegal guns found in the storage building, then said, "But the sight I'm not likely to forget for a long time, if ever, is seeing Andrew Olsson holding a pistol to his brother Eric's head before pointing it at me. At that moment I was sure I might be next if I didn't think fast. Didn't need to. In a split second Sheriff Ferris and Eric Olsson teamed up to surprise the hell out of me. While Eric managed to lurch forward with a twist that knocked his brother off balance, Sheriff Ferris finished the job by slamming into the two of them from behind. As Andrew lost his footing, his right arm flew up and out to the side, one finger inadvertently pressing hard enough on the pistol trigger to release the safety. The guy shot himself in the side of his head. And, as you know, a bullet in the brain will kill you every time . . . lucky for me, I guess."

Again the room was quiet.

"Who would have expected that," said Lew softly.

"That reminds me," said Bruce before she could continue, "no ballistics in yet on the bullet that shattered Doc's window—"

"The one aimed at me?" asked Lew with a wry smile.

"Yep. That's the one," said Bruce. "Hope to hear something soon."

"Anyone have more to add?" asked Lew.

After a soft shuffling of feet and papers and no one speaking up, she said, "Thank you, everyone. If you don't mind, I'm heading out. I have a meeting with Connie Steadman and Eric Olsson shortly. I'll be sure to let you know if they have anything new to add."

She studied the serious faces around the table. "We got a lot done, people, and I want to thank everyone.

"Oh, one more thing," she said, getting to her feet, "Does four-thirty this afternoon at the Prairie River sound good? Dani, you can come along to watch and help me hand out treats. And, Pete, I demand you not leave Loon Lake until you have at least one brookie released. And that is nonnegotiable."

As laughter broke out, Lew left the room smiling.

CHAPTER

32

"Good morning, Lew," said Connie, opening the front door of the Olsson's log mansion before Lew could knock. "Thank you for coming so soon. If you'll follow me back to the kitchen, Eric is brewing us some coffee."

"Good morning, Sheriff Ferris. Coffee?" asked Eric who was standing by a coffee maker on the side counter. He held out an empty mug.

"I'd love some," said Lew. "Black, please, Eric. How is your father doing? This has to be hard on him."

"He seems to be doing okay. Connie and I drove him to town to have breakfast with an old childhood friend of his. You know, growing up my dad spent his summers here and has a friend or two from those days—old guys still alive. Who'd have expected *that*." He smiled then said, "Thank you for asking," he said as he handed her a mug of coffee.

"While Dad seemed okay this morning, I'm not sure he understands most of what has been happening."

"Most?" asked Lew after accepting the full mug and taking a chair at the table.

"He is in worse shape mentally than I realized even though Connie has been keeping me informed. Not sure if it's Alzheimer's or dementia, but whichever, it's catching up with him. He was pretty good up until a few months ago but since he turns ninety soon, I shouldn't be surprised, and it does help explain some things."

"Speaking of explaining," said Connie, "I still wish I had said more to you that night I ran into you at the restaurant." Looking dejected, she shook her head.

"Me, too," said Lew. "I've been thinking about the words you used: 'They know who you are.' That's all you said and since then, especially after the shooting at Dr. Osborne's house, I can't help wondering if it *was* a warning, if you knew that someone *was* after me. Were you aware that Andrew was thinking about or planning to—"

"Oh, gosh, no," said Connie, shaking her head so emphatically Lew felt sorry for her.

"What I meant was *I know someone who is furious with you, Lewellyn*. But I meant anger. That's all. So let me tell you how it was I knew only that at the time.

"A few days earlier, I had, as part of my job serving as an E.P. agent for Eric's father, gone along with Grant and Andy when they drove over to meet with the owner of Ralph's Sporting Goods. Grant had a number of guns that gun collectors, customers of his, were hoping he could sell for them. He had taken some guns in on trade for his antique guns but they were not antiques or anything he wanted to sell on his site. He was trying to keep his business focused on the antique guns."

"My father has a family history of buying and selling rifles and other hunting gear through Ralph Stanton," said Eric, referring to the owner of the sporting goods shop. "And, just so you know, this morning I got my dad to agree to shut down his website. You can't be dealing guns, even antique guns, at his age and in his condition. Sorry for interrupting, Connie," said Eric with a wave of apology. "Please—finish what you were saying."

"So I'm at Ralph's Sporting Goods that day with Grant and Andy," said Connie, "and I'm standing back, just listening when Grant shows Ralph two semi-automatic AR-15s and asks him to resell the guns. In retrospect, I realize those guns were from Andy, not any of Grant's customers.

"Well, Ralph is quite taken aback. He tells Grant and I quote, 'I'm not licensed in this state to sell guns like these—and I never will be. The kind of people who buy AK-47s are not the customers I want. Guns like this are not for hunting, Grant. Are you out of your mind? If our county sheriff, Lew Ferris, got wind of my handling these—she'd have me behind bars so fast. No, I won't resell AK-47s for you or,' and he turned to Andy, 'you either. You two should know better. Now take those damn things and leave. Get 'em out of here. Now.'"

"Connie," asked Lew, "did you know beforehand that Grant and Andrew were bringing those guns in that day?"

"No, the guns were in Andy's truck and I did not see them, nor was there a mention of them until we met up with Andy that day at Ralph's Sporting Goods. When we got back here afterward that day, I told Grant he better let his son know that getting into any dealings with those guns would be a disaster."

"But Andy was already very involved, I think," said Eric, chiming in.

"Yes," said Connie, "and here's what happened next. That day that you and your deputies took over the old cabin in the Robideaux Forest is the same day that Andy drove back here demanding his dad let him sell guns through his antique gun website. I was in the storage building helping Grant with some paperwork when Andy stormed in swearing and cursing. He kept repeating 'that horrible Ferris woman is ruining my business. She's making it *impossible* for me to do business! And, Dad, that's not all. She's one of the people trying to shut down sports gambling, too.'"

"He was furious with you, Lew, and that's why I said what I did when I saw you. I wanted you to know there was a very angry person out there—someone who might go to your board of supervisors, file a complaint, whatever.

"Today, I feel so bad," said Connie, "if only I had said more. Like given you his name and more background, but I had no idea Andy would go as far as he did."

"None of us had any idea," said Eric, reaching over to pat Connie's hand. "You think I was expecting my kid brother to pull a gun on me?"

"I wonder what made Andy think he could get away with selling those guns," said Lew, "those and the other machine guns we found? And the ghost guns? We found several of those, too. Highly illegal. Whether it would be me or the FBI, we'd all be on to him eventually," she said. "I, for one, was determined to find out who was using the old logging cabin for trafficking."

"My take on it," said Eric, "is this. First, my brother has never been the brightest bear in the woods—"

"Most criminals aren't," said Lew, interrupting with a grim smile.

"—and second, he likely figured he'd make a couple hundred thousand bucks and scoot out of the country before anyone got on to him. His efforts at sports gambling have been a miserable failure, too. I'll bet he was thinking: 'Sell the guns, take the cash and head on down to Mexico.'"

CHAPTER

33

CONNIE WALKED LEW to the front door, where she paused, looked down at the floor and was quiet.

"What?" asked Lew, "did I forget something?"

"Oh, no," said Connie, giving her a sheepish smile, "it's just that I have a strange question for you. . . ."

"No strange questions," said Lew, "try me."

"Any chance," Connie grimaced before she asked, raising her eyebrows, "you'd be looking for an experienced detective one of these days? Like one with twenty-five years of experience?"

Lew grinned. "Try me," she said, "I've been interviewing for someone to manage my new hires, someone who's, you know, been around the block in Wisconsin and other states, maybe had some private security experience, too. Someone who might give me a call tomorrow and we can talk things over."

The two women shook hands, each with a quiet smile as they walked off.

* * *

Twenty minutes later, as she was letting herself into her cruiser to return to her office, Lew's personal cell phone rang. "Bruce, here, Sheriff. Got the ballistics in on the two bullets that we pulled out of the muskie on the wall at Doc Osborne's. As I expected, it is a match to bullets fired from the deer rifle that we found yesterday in Andrew Olsson's pickup. No question he's the guy who shot at the Osborne house two nights ago when you were sitting in the living room behind that big picture window. No question whatsoever. A copy of the documentation is on your desk. Just put it there."

"Thank you, Bruce," said Lew. "It's a relief to have that confirmed. And thank you for taking such good care of the muskie." They both chuckled.

CHAPTER

34

LEW TURNED LEFT to drive Nellie, her trusty fishing truck, down the rocky lane to the clearing along the Prairie River where she liked to park. As usual, when Nellie bounced hard over the rocks, Osborne held tight to the door handle on his side. To Lew's surprise she saw Rob Mason's van parked with its doors open and two figures seated on nearby boulders. The two were in the midst of pulling wading boots on over their waders. As she pulled up next to their van, Rob and Ben looked up and waved.

"What the heck are you two up to?" she asked after jumping out of Nellie and walking toward them with a smile of surprise. Osborne, meanwhile, was busy pulling his waders and rod holder out of the back of her truck.

"About an hour ago, after Ben got home from school, he and I were mulling over this good weather," said Rob, getting to his feet as he adjusted the straps of his waders, "and Ben said that ever since watching you the other day, he'd like to try casting my fly rod again."

"Sheriff Ferris," said Ben as he moved to stand by his dad, "I made a few bucks on our muskie tournament. Do you still give casting lessons, and how much do you charge?"

Lew laughed, "Oh, golly. Well, I do try to get some time in on the trout stream, but *lessons*?"

She saw Ben's face fall as if worried he was about to get a negative answer.

"I give a lesson now and then. But no charge. You save your share of the prize money for going to college, Ben. And if you're lucky enough to win a scholarship then send a few bucks to Trout Unlimited to help protect our brookies and our streams. How's that for a deal?"

Right then a familiar SUV pulled up and out jumped Bruce Peters. A second later, Pete Cooke climbed out of the passenger seat. "Hey, Sheriff," called Pete as he stood up to look over the car door. "Tell this bozo to give it up on the bamboo, will you? He's spending too much money on the damn thing."

"Listen, you guys," said Lew, walking toward the two men as they started unloading their waders and rod holders, "I have an idea. You two battle it out in the stream tonight. The one who hooks the first brookie can allege that his way—whether bamboo or graphite—is the right way. Sound fair?"

Pete and Bruce exchanged looks, then Pete said, "Nope. That doesn't work for me. I'm a graphite guy, like you, Sheriff. It's all about the light weight and fast recovery, period. Doesn't matter who gets the first fish—or how many fish. What matters is what feels right as I cast, what works for me on my double haul. Personal choice."

"He might be right," said Bruce with a wince and bounce of his brows. "Ease over elegance." Lew knew he hated to concede, but she suspected he'd been practicing with his borrowed bamboo rod ever since they'd talked. Likely he'd been disappointed but resisted admitting he might be wrong, especially after extolling the virtues of bamboo so loudly.

"Excuse me, folks, but I'm heading up stream before it gets any darker," said Osborne from the streambank. He gave a wave and stepped into the water.

"Wait, Doc," said Bruce, "before you get started, I want to let you know that Ray is hosting us for walleye at his place later. You and Lew are expected, too." With a wave and a grin, Osborne set off.

Lew turned to Ben, who had been standing nearby, listening. He had assembled one of his dad's fly rods and stood waiting. She could see that he was hoping she might take him up on his request for a lesson. Rob had entered the stream with his rod ready but he had paused, waiting to see what Lew would do.

"Okay, Ben, let's start down here," said Lew, pointing to the water's edge. "I'm going to show you the right grip and how to do a roll cast. You'll know then if you're likely to be comfortable with a fly rod. And if you are, I'll give you another lesson or two before it snows but

I'm going to encourage you and your dad to take the time, both of you, to plan a long weekend next spring at the Wulff School of Fly Fishing in the New York Catskills. It'll be a fun drive east and a terrific all-around introduction to fly fishing. That's where I learned everything I know. And, Rob, you can stand a lesson or two yourself, right?"

"Yeah, guess so," said Rob with a pleased look on his face and a chuckle as he started upstream.

* * *

Late that night after an hour and a half in the stream followed by delicious sauteed walleye and bad jokes at Ray's, Osborne and Lew lay side by side under the blankets on his bed. "Doc," said Lew, her voice soft, "that gunshot changed my thinking. It could have been my last night here. . . ."

"Don't obsess over that, Lewellyn," said Osborne, turning onto one side to gaze at her, "it wasn't your time. Even my big ol' muskie survived. All he's got is a couple tiny holes beneath his left gill from those bullets.

"Don't change the subject," said Lew, reaching over to give him a gentle punch in the shoulder. "How many times have you asked me to marry you?"

"Um . . . seventeen. Why? You want me to ask again?"

"Nope. If the offer still stands, I accept."

Without a second's hesitation, Osborne asked, "On Halloween or Thanksgiving weekend?"

"Oh, let's do Halloween. Sounds fun."

"You know Ray will insist on saying a few words. . . ."

"Now that could be dangerous."

* * *

Half an hour later, pulling the comforter up to their chins, the two fell asleep. A pale autumn moon shone through the window above their heads, which was slightly ajar. An owl hooted. The rustling of a chipmunk could be heard. And the wolves? Watching.

EPILOGUE

AFTER THE "GETAWAY" from the site where John McKenzie had deliberately wrecked his fellow club member's expensive wolf-watching equipment out of anger, he drove in fuming silence.

They had driven more than an hour, clearly not heading to the lodge where they had booked their stay, before Miriam dared ask a question. "Hon, where are we going?"

"Robideaux Forest," said John with a grunt. "An old buddy of mine from med school said he's hunted birds there and seen lots of wolves. Now shut up and let me drive."

Miriam obeyed. She pulled out her AirPods and plugged in to listen to a new novel recommended by her book club. After an hour, she tilted her passenger seat back and fell sound asleep.

She woke to find the car stopped but running in a clearing in front of a small log cabin. John was out of the car but she could see no sign of him. Assuming he had entered the small cabin, she rolled down her window. She could hear voices that seemed to come from inside the building. Right then a black pickup pulled up alongside their car and a scruffy-looking teenager hopped out. He reached into the back seat of the pickup and pulled out a large rifle, which he carried into the cabin.

The voices grew louder and she could make out John starting to shout that, "This is public land and I have every right to drive back there! You just try to stop me. . . ."

Before he had finished shouting, she saw him backing out of the cabin, now silent, with a tall, dark-haired man pushing him in the chest with a large handgun.

"All right, all right, I'll leave," said John turning to walk toward Miriam and the car.

"Stop right there," ordered the man with the gun. "You"—he waved at Miriam still sitting in the front seat of their car—"You, out. Get out. Now."

Miriam, shoving the AirPods into her jacket pocket, did as she was told without a word.

The man marched them a short distance down the path behind the cabin. "Kneel," he ordered.

They did, awkwardly. John opened his mouth, but before he could say a word, Miriam said, "John, shut up!" With surprise on his face, he did. Miriam knew there was no way out of this, that he'd this time gotten them into something he couldn't bluff or bully his way out of, something with no happy ending, and she didn't want to listen to him.

She looked away from him, up at the sky, and thought of their son, Brian, and his wife, Riley, and their grandchild, with love and sad regret. *If only she had stood up to John long ago*, she thought. *If only she had had the courage to leave.* But at least her family was safe. They would mourn, but they would be spared the fallout from John's tantrum and his destroying Harry's wolf-watching equipment—no repercussions, no fall from grace, no arrest. And her will and last wishes were in place.

The gun barked once, and then again. Before she toppled to the ground, Miriam had time for just one thought: *At least I had the last word for once.*

ACKNOWLEDGMENTS

A HEARTFELT THANK-YOU TO everyone who has helped *The Wolves Are Watching* read easy, look good and make my readers happy. My first thank-you goes to Ben LeRoy, my long-time friend and editor who has always been there with excellent advice and support.

Next is a warm thank-you to Sara J. Henry for her impeccable editing and good humor. Then a shout-out to Thaisheemarie Fantauzzi Pérez, who has kept me in touch with the Crooked Lane team that created the striking, haunting book jacket and marketing plan, which makes all the difference in the publishing world. This team includes my expert copy editor, Debbie Stone, and the talented designer, Nebojsa Zoric. None of this could have happened without the meticulous guidance of Dulce Botello and others in senior management—Crooked Lane Books is the best.

Finally, thank-you to Christopher Combemale, my agent and good friend at Sterling Lord Literistic Inc.

And thank-you to my family—Mike Mack, Nicole, Ryan, and Steve Melcher, who, with their families, have been my loving supporters throughout my publishing career.

And so it goes: Murder, mystery, and excellent fishing in the Northwoods of Wisconsin.